YORK NOTES

Pride and Prejudice

Jane Austen

Notes by Paul Pascoe

 Longman   York Press

YORK PRESS
322 Old Brompton Road, London SW5 9JH

Pearson Education Limited
Edinburgh Gate, Harlow,
Essex CM20 2JE, United Kingdom
Associated companies, branches and representatives throughout the world

First published 1998
Fourth impression 2000

ISBN 0-582-36838-3

Designed by Vicki Pacey, Trojan Horse, London
Illustrated by Susan Scott
Phototypeset by Gem Graphics, Trenance, Mawgan Porth, Cornwall
Colour reproduction and film output by Spectrum Colour
Produced by Pearson Education China Limited, Hong Kong

CONTENTS

PREFACE

York Notes are designed to give you a broader perspective on works of literature studied at GCSE and equivalent levels. We have carried out extensive research into the needs of the modern literature student prior to publishing this new edition. Our research showed that no existing series fully met students' requirements. Rather than present a single authoritative approach, we have provided alternative viewpoints, empowering students to reach their own interpretations of the text. York Notes provide a close examination of the work and include biographical and historical background, summaries, glossaries, analyses of characters, themes, structure and language, cultural connections and literary terms.

If you look at the Contents page you will see the structure for the series. However, there's no need to read from the beginning to the end as you would with a novel, play, poem or short story. Use the Notes in the way that suits you. Our aim is to help you with your understanding of the work, not to dictate how you should learn.

York Notes are written by English teachers and examiners, with an expert knowledge of the subject. They show you how to succeed in coursework and examination assignments, guiding you through the text and offering practical advice. Questions and comments will extend, test and reinforce your knowledge. Attractive colour design and illustrations improve clarity and understanding, making these Notes easy to use and handy for quick reference.

York Notes are ideal for:
- Essay writing
- Exam preparation
- Class discussion

The author of these Notes is Paul Pascoe, who has been a Chief and Principal Examiner in English since 1974. Author of a number of textbooks for Secondary pupils, he was until recently Head of English at Formby High Comprehensive School.

The edition used in these Notes is the Penguin Classics Edition, 1996, edited with an introduction and notes by Vivien Jones.

Health Warning: **This study guide will enhance your understanding, but should not replace the reading of the original text and/or study in class.**

PART ONE

INTRODUCTION

HOW TO STUDY A NOVEL

You have bought this book because you wanted to study a novel on your own. This may supplement classwork.

- You will need to read the novel several times. Start by reading it quickly for pleasure, then read it slowly and carefully. Further readings will generate new ideas and help you to memorise the details of the story.
- Make careful notes on themes, plot and characters of the novel. The plot will change some of the characters. Who changes?
- The novel may not present events chronologically. Does the novel you are reading begin at the beginning of the story or does it contain flashbacks and a muddled time sequence? Can you think why?
- How is the story told? Is it narrated by one of the characters or by an all-seeing ('omniscient') narrator?
- Does the same person tell the story all the way through? Or do we see the events through the minds and feelings of a number of different people.
- Which characters does the narrator like? Which characters do you like or dislike? Do your sympathies change during the course of the book? Why? When?
- Any piece of writing (including your notes and essays) is the result of thousands of choices. No book had to be written in just one way: the author could have chosen other words, other phrases, other characters, other events. How could the author of your novel have written the story differently? If events were recounted by a minor character how would this change the novel?

Studying on your own requires self-discipline and a carefully thought-out work plan in order to be effective. Good luck.

Rather after the manner of her novels, Jane Austen's life is devoid of dramatic incident but richly textured in its fine detail. She was born at Steventon in Hampshire on 16 December 1775, the daughter of the Reverend George Austen, rector of the small country parishes of Steventon and Deane. Her father was a kindly and scholarly man who nurtured Jane in her early reading and writing. In 1782, Jane and her elder sister, Cassandra, were sent away to a family friend and later attended a boarding school in Reading run by amiable, wooden-legged Mrs Latourenelle who apparently could talk of nothing but the theatre. In 1797 she returned to Steventon where she was able to steep herself in her father's considerable library.

Jane was one of a closely-knit family.

The Austen family was large; apart from Cassandra, to whom she was especially close, she had five brothers who eventually produced no fewer than nine sets of in-laws! By all accounts, the Austen family were a happy circle and the Rectory was rarely short of activity. Life at Steventon was further enlivened by the arrival in 1797 of George Austen's rather giddy niece. She loved acting and provided an extra stimulus to the Austen family theatricals which flourished in the Rectory's barn. Amateur theatricals play an important part in her novel *Mansfield Park*. Although Steventon was very remote, there were endless opportunities to mix socially and observe human behaviour in close detail. As she later wrote, 'three or four families in a Country Village is the very thing to work on'.

She produced a flow of mischievous **satire** and **parody** (see Literary Terms), with the cheap **romantic novel** (see Literary Terms) the main butt of her humour. The subtitle of *Love and Friendship* – 'Deceived in Friendship and Betrayed in Love' – which she wrote when she was fourteen, provides us with the flavour of the sentimental fiction which she was satirising. Of her

more mature work, *Northanger Abbey* still serves as an
entertaining send-up of pulp fiction. She spent the first
twenty-five years of her life at Steventon but like her
heroines, she occasionally travelled further afield. In
1801 the family moved to Bath, a fashionable city she
knew well but never really liked. In 1806 Jane's father
died and the family moved to Southampton and three
years later moved to the small Hampshire village of
Chawton. She lived there with her mother, her sister
Cassandra and their friend Martha Lloyd.

*Jane's success
and early
death*

At Chawton she wrote her major novels and became a
favourite aunt to her numerous nephews and nieces.
Her first success was *Sense and Sensibility* which was
published in 1811 for which she received £140. Two
years later a 'lop't and crop't' version of an earlier
unpublished novel, *First Impressions*, emerged as *Pride
and Prejudice*. *Mansfield Park* followed in 1814 and
Emma was published in 1816. *Persuasion* and
Northanger Abbey, which she had written in 1788–9,
were published posthumously. In 1817 she contracted
what is believed to be Addison's Disease, a rare
glandular condition. Good humoured as ever, she
admitted wryly that 'Sickness is a Dangerous
Indulgence at my time of life'. In May 1817 she was
moved to Winchester attended by her brother Henry
and her nephew William. On 18 July 1817, she died in
Cassandra's arms. She is buried in Winchester
Cathedral. On 29 July 1817, Cassandra wrote of the
funeral: 'Never was human being more sincerely
mourned by those who attended her remains than was
this dear creature'.

CONTEXT & SETTING

Jane Austen's novels contain little description and few
references to background details. Nevertheless, Jane
Austen presents us with a fully imagined world. In her

novels the general context is assumed rather than
stated, so it is helpful for the modern reader to bring to
the novels some grasp of the kind of world that would
have been familiar to her characters.

Social
structures

The division of society into upper, middle and lower
classes did not emerge until well into the nineteenth
century. Jane Austen would have partitioned society
rather differently into aristocracy, gentry and common
people. Most of Jane Austen's characters are members
of the gentry. They were largely a landowning class, but
included others, such as Anglican clergy. Tradespeople
were excluded. There were also divisions within the
gentry. Fitzwilliam Darcy, in contrast to Mr Bennet,
comes from an ancient family and, although not titled,
commands a status above that of many of the nobility,
such as Lady Catherine.

By the end of the eighteenth century, however, the
social fabric was already changing. In particular, the
distinction between landed gentry and city tradespeople
had become blurred. Darcy's 'rejection' of Lady
Catherine and his intimacy with the Gardiners is a kind
of symbolic reflection of these changes. The
eighteenth-century economist, Adam Smith, had
observed that 'Merchants are commonly ambitious of
becoming country gentlemen'. Sir William Lucas is a
case in point. Conversely, many country landlords were
investing in trade and the growing financial institutions.
What is more, new, more efficient farming methods,
such as the use of Jethro Tull's drill, were involving
many landlords in business and trade.

Manners and
values

The title 'gentleman' accorded one social privilege but it
also assumed certain standards of behaviour. Those
standards found their outward expression in strict codes
of conduct. There were clear procedures regarding
visiting, introductions, forms of address, social
conversation, order of precedence and the formal

relationships between the sexes. Raw emotions were never to be displayed openly in public, although one's meaning could be made absolutely clear while maintaining the outward civilities. Elizabeth's parting remarks to Wickham are a good example of this.

The art of conversation performed an important social role. In part, it was a kind of verbal game of squash, in which the participants would strenuously strive to keep a point alive. Some, like Bingley, could not stand the pace. In theory, the outward formalities and civilities reflected inner values and moral standards. The reality, however, fell short of the ideal and Jane Austen constantly exposes the mismatch between the social and moral scales.

Marriage and wealth

Among the well-to-do at least, marriage was much more like a business transaction than it is today. The great families saw marriage as a means of forming alliances that would sustain the position of power. Even among lesser families, marriage contracts could include complex financial conditions. However, by the end of the eighteenth century, young people exercised more freedom of choice; arranged marriages, such as that proposed by Lady Catherine, had already died out by Jane Austen's day.

For women, marriage was often the only means of social improvement. Romance apart, Elizabeth is successful because she has secured upward mobility and security for herself and her family.

The question of money forms a foil to romance; Jane Austen was never less than a realist in this respect. It is difficult to draw absolute parallels with today's values, but Mr Bennet's £2,000 per annum or Darcy's £10,000 per annum needs to be seen in light of other typical incomes. A successful tradesman like Mr Gardiner might expect to earn £700 per annum (some, of course became very rich indeed), whilst a shopkeeper might aspire to about £150 a year. A tenant farmer might receive about £120, whilst an agricultural worker had to survive on about £30 a year. To run Bingley's carriage alone, would have needed an income of between £800 to £1000 a year

Setting

Although by 1811, London's population exceeded one million for the first time, England was still a predominantly rural society. Although no specific details are given, Longbourn will have comprised the house, a farm and associated houses. Mr Bennet will probably have employed an agent to run his estate. Pemberley will have been a community in its own right with many dependent on it for their livelihood. It probably will have supported an estate village and, as well as the 'Home Farm' belonging to the house itself, there will be a number of outlying farms. Major landowners, like Mr Darcy, often had the sole power to appoint clergy to the churches which they controlled. These 'livings' could be very lucrative and were much sought after. In Jane Austen's time the Church was one of the major professions that combined high status with a comfortable and secure existence.

The arrangement of rooms plays quite a significant role in Jane Austen's novels. All but the smallest houses would sport a parlour or day room; some larger houses, such as Rosings, had a breakfast parlour which was also a morning sitting room. Dinner was served in the dining room and after dessert the ladies would withdraw to the drawing room to be joined later by the gentlemen. The larger houses such as Netherfield had drawing rooms sufficiently large to accommodate dancing, or even an indoor stroll.

During the eighteenth century, dinner was served as early as four-thirty but in common with the growing trend, the Bennets dine between six-thirty and seven.

Elizabeth and the Gardiners visit Pemberley for luncheon, a new meal intended to bridge the growing gap between breakfast and dinner.

Social gatherings were particularly important in Jane Austen's day. The ball, the musical evening and the card-table were at the centre of social life and could bring together a surprisingly diverse range of people. Communities such as Meryton would raise money by subscription to support public dances or 'assemblies'. The local inn was often the venue. There was an increasing trend, however, towards the staging of private balls at large country houses. Either way, such occasions were seen as an opportunity for matchmaking.

By the end of the nineteenth century, the better off were significantly more mobile. New 'turnpike' roads made it possible to travel easily from town to country. But transport was expensive; very few could maintain their own carriage. Mr Bennet's horses, for instance, are often needed for farm work. Except for the likes of Darcy and Bingley, a journey of any distance was an adventure. In Jane Austen's novels a change of place, such as the shift of scene to Hunsford or to Pemberley, invariably signals an important development in the plot.

Historical and literary background Jane Austen's life coincided with a period of political upheaval. Revolutionary cries of personal liberty and freedom had swept through Europe and extended to the New World, precipitating the United States Declaration of Independence in 1776 and the French Revolution in 1789. For most of Jane Austen's adult life Britain was at war with France.

In the field of the arts, the **Romantic movement** (see Literary Terms), which stressed the importance of imagination and personal emotion, was approaching its height. The poets, Wordsworth and Coleridge, the painter, J.M.W. Turner, the composer, Beethoven and Jane Austen were all born within five years of one another.

However, there is barely a hint of these tumultuous times in Jane Austen's work. She preferred to scrutinise the emotional ripples within a comparatively settled and familiar society than to chart the tempestuous seas of distant revolution. Artistically, she drew her strength from the example of the great eighteenth-century prose writers, such as Dr Johnson, whose cool, well-ordered, witty and incisive observations on life formed the basis of her style. The passion of **Romanticism** (see Literary Terms) did not inspire her. In fact, in her last novel, *Persuasion*, the heroine is found discouraging a lovelorn young man from reading the emotionally charged poetry of the day.

Contemporary writers of romantic novels were an influence on Jane Austen.

She was, however, influenced by a band of mainly women writers of **romantic novels** (see Literary Terms) with titles like *Belinda*, *The Old Manor House* and *Almeyda*, *Queen of Grenada*. Today, names such as Fanny Burney, Maria Edgeworth, Mrs Radcliffe, Charlotte Smith and Sophia Lee are perhaps familiar only to the specialist but they were immensely popular at the beginning of the nineteenth century. Jane Austen chose to build her plots along the lines of popular fiction but turned them sharply to her own ends (see Structure).

PART TWO

SUMMARIES

GENERAL SUMMARY

Chapters 1–12

Mr and Mrs Bennet live at Longbourn in Hertfordshire, near to the small town of Meryton. Mrs Bennet, who is a very silly woman, is obsessed with finding husbands for her five daughters. She is partly justified because Mr Bennet's estate is 'entailed' so that, on his death, it will pass to his cousin, Mr Collins, and his daughters will inherit nothing.

Her prayers seem about to be answered when a rich young bachelor, Charles Bingley, takes up residence at Netherfield, a nearby estate, bringing with him his two sisters and his wealthy friend, Fitzwilliam Darcy. At the town ball, Bingley, who is liked by all, immediately falls in love with the eldest daughter, Jane, while Darcy is attracted to her vivacious sister, Elizabeth. Like most of the company, however, Elizabeth finds Darcy proud and disagreeable.

Elizabeth has further opportunities to observe the Bingleys and Darcy at close quarters when she stays with Jane at Netherfield. She has some animated conversations with Darcy that confirm her view that he is arrogant and intolerant of others. He on the other hand finds himself 'bewitched' by her lively spirit. Elizabeth also doubts the sincerity Caroline Bingley, whom she finds 'supercilious'.

Chapters 13–23

Mr Bennet receives an extraordinary letter from his cousin, the Reverend Mr Collins, announcing his imminent arrival and hinting at his intention of marrying one of the sisters. He turns out to be an opinionated, officious oaf who is constantly showing servile deference to Lady Catherine de Bourgh who had presented him with his living and who also

happens to be Darcy's aunt. Meanwhile, there is
another arrival in the district, George Wickham, a
young officer in the Militia which has been garrisoned
in Meryton. He quickly makes a favourable impression
on Elizabeth who finds his company charming and
entertaining. He claims that in the past Darcy has
treated him most unjustly. Elizabeth is shocked by
Wickham's story which serves to intensify her dislike
of Darcy.

A ball is arranged at Netherfield but Wickham fails to
appear. Elizabeth believes that Darcy is responsible for
his absence and refuses to believe warnings that she
should not accept Wickham at face value. Elizabeth's
evening ends in misery when she has to witness
members of her family behaving with embarrassing
vulgarity.

Mr Collins duly proposes to Elizabeth and though
hurt by her firm refusal quickly transfers his attentions
to Elizabeth's closest friend, Charlotte Lucas, who
immediately accepts his offer of marriage. Elizabeth is
shocked, feeling that Charlotte has demeaned herself,
but promises to visit her in Kent.

The Bingleys and Darcy suddenly decide to quit
Netherfield for London. Elizabeth suspects that
Bingley's sisters and Darcy want to separate him from
Jane.

Chapters
24–38

Jane is invited to London to stay with her aunt and
uncle, the Gardiners. There are brief hopes that Jane
will meet Bingley once again but Caroline Bingley's
offhand treatment of Jane make it clear that she does
not wish the acquaintance to be renewed. Jane is quietly
heartbroken, whilst Elizabeth is depressed for her
sister's sake.

Elizabeth fulfils her promise to visit Charlotte and
is saddened that her friend seems quite satisfied by her

comfortable but loveless existence. She is appalled by Lady Catherine's domineering and insolently arrogant manner, so much so that she actually welcomes the arrival of Darcy and his cousin Colonel Fitzwilliam. Darcy is so captivated by Elizabeth that he suddenly proposes to her, at the same time making it clear how he has had to put aside their differences in rank. Elizabeth is furious and refuses him on the grounds that his proud attitude is ungentlemanly, that he had deprived her sister of her happiness and that he had mistreated Wickham. The next day Darcy hands Elizabeth a long letter justifying his behaviour and exposing Wickham as a liar.

Elizabeth is forced to acknowledge the truth of Darcy's explanation, including his remarks on her family's ill-breeding.

Chapters 39–50

On returning to Longbourn, Elizabeth is ashamed that her father has permitted the flighty Lydia to follow the Militia to Brighton. She is relieved to escape with her aunt and uncle on a trip to Derbyshire. Believing the family to be away she agrees to visit Pemberley, Darcy's great estate. She is astonished to learn from the housekeeper how much Darcy is loved and respected by all the local people. Her astonishment is even greater when, returning unexpectedly, Darcy proves entirely affable and especially courteous towards her aunt and uncle.

Elizabeth begins to realise that she could love Darcy but her dreams are shattered when news arrives that Lydia has eloped with Wickham. On returning to Longbourn, the situation seems hopeless. Elizabeth doubts that Wickham has any intention of marrying Lydia and the visits of 'sympathetic' neighbours only serve to emphasise the disgrace and leave Elizabeth in despair. However, before long Mr Gardiner writes to say that he has come to an arrangement with

Wickham and the couple are to be married. Mrs Bennet is ecstatic.

An unrepentant and Lydia lets slip that Darcy was at the wedding. In response to Elizabeth's urgent enquiry about the truth of the matter, Mrs Gardiner explains that it was in fact Darcy who enforced the marriage. Overcome with gratitude and respect, Elizabeth dares to wonder whether Darcy did it for her.

Soon after Lydia and Wickham leave, Bingley and Darcy arrive. Bingley clearly still loves Jane but Darcy behaves stiffly and says very little. Before long, Bingley proposes to Jane and there is joy all round.

Lady Catherine makes a surprise visit and demands that Elizabeth should deny that she and Darcy are engaged. When he learns of Elizabeth's refusal, Darcy is encouraged to propose again. This time Elizabeth accepts.

DETAILED SUMMARIES

CHAPTERS 1–6

Mr Bennet's cool wit (see Literary Terms) is a foil to Mrs Bennet's giddy chatter.

The novel opens in the Bennet family home, which comprises the house and village of Longbourn, lying about a mile outside the small country town of Meryton. Mr and Mrs Bennet have five daughters and we are immediately made aware that Mrs Bennet's one concern in life is to see them married. She becomes increasingly frustrated and agitated at Mr Bennet's seeming indifference at the appearance in the neighbourhood of an eligible bachelor, Mr Bingley. Without Mr Bennet first paying a formal visit, the chance of making this vital acquaintance will be lost. For his part, Mr Bennet is content to tease his wife and express good-natured amusement at yet another demonstration of her 'nerves'.

We see Mrs Bennet's instantaneous changes of mood for the first time.

In point of fact, Mr Bennet has fulfilled his obligations and already visited Mr Bingley but he extracts as much enjoyment as he can from keeping his family in ignorance. Mrs Bennet continues to sulk, despite Elizabeth's reassurances, until her despondency vanishes instantly on hearing the truth.

Mr Bingley performs the customary courtesy of returning Mr Bennet's visit but the ladies are able to gain only a fleeting glimpse of him from an upstairs window. Mrs Bennet pictures one of her daughter's happily married in Netherfield, the country house that Bingley has rented, but her immediate plans of matchmaking are dashed by the news that Bingley has returned to London to bring down a 'large party for the ball'. In fact, he brings only five: his two sisters, his brother-in-law, Mr Hurst and a friend, Mr Darcy. The ball in question is one of the regular public 'assemblies', popular at the time, at which people could meet, converse, see and be seen. Consequently Bingley and his party come under close scrutiny. Bingley proves to be affable and outgoing. He rapidly gains everyone's approval but his friend, Darcy, handsome though he is, appears cold, distant and unfriendly. Indeed, Elizabeth overhears him expressing his thorough dislike of the occasion in general and poor impression of her in

Everyone takes a prejudiced dislike of Mr Darcy.

particular. Elizabeth laughs off the insult by relating the incident to her friends with great amusement but Mrs Bennet is able only to 'quite detest the man'. Otherwise, the ball is deemed a great success and Mrs Bennet returns home, joyful at the fact that Mr Bingley had found Jane 'quite beautiful' and actually danced with her twice.

Jane and Elizabeth compare their impressions of Bingley and his sisters. Jane is favourably impressed, but whilst conceding that Bingley is undoubtedly 'agreeable', Elizabeth prefers to withhold her final

THE BENNETS, AN ELIGIBLE BACHELOR AND HIS PROUD FRIEND

judgement, feeling that her elder sister is too ready to see only the good in everybody. Furthermore, Elizabeth is less impressed by Bingley's sisters whom, for all their elegance and refinement, she finds too full of a sense of their own superiority.

The Bingleys' background is made known.

We learn that Bingley and his sisters are extremely wealthy and that he may be seeking to purchase a country estate. We are also told of Bingley's dependence on his good friend Darcy's judgement and superior intelligence. The two men's characters are contrasted through their reactions to the ball. Bingley was delighted at the pleasant company and the exceptionally pretty girls, whereas Darcy found the company dull and unfashionable although he granted that Miss Bennet (Jane) was tolerably pretty, despite smiling too much.

The title 'Miss' was reserved for the eldest unmarried daughter in a family.

The Bennets are visited by some of the children of their close friends, Sir William and Lady Lucas. Sir William is newly risen in the world having made a modest fortune in trade, but is very anxious to forget his background and prove himself a true country gentleman. Although he is uncommonly proud of his title, he and his wife are a naturally pleasant and friendly couple.

Mr Darcy's
character is
assessed.

Charlotte Lucas is Elizabeth's closest friend whose views on love and marriage emerge, during the course of the novel, as very different from those of Elizabeth. Several opinions of Mr Darcy are offered. Mrs Bennet finds him thoroughly disagreeable and 'ate up with pride'. Jane, who sees the best in everyone, suggests that he is naturally shy and reticent. Charlotte, however, feels that in view of his wealth and background, he has much to be proud about. Elizabeth admits that her pride has been hurt. The bookish Mary offers some thoughts on the distinction between pride and vanity, which everybody ignores.

Acquaintances deepen as a result of an exchange of visits between Longbourn and Netherfield. Bingley's sisters are prepared to entertain an interest in Jane and Elizabeth but find Mrs Bennet 'intolerable' and wholly disregard the other sisters. For her part, Elizabeth continues to find their attitude patronising and feels that their apparent warmth is entirely owing to Bingley's feelings for Jane. Jane is clearly falling in love with Bingley but Elizabeth and Charlotte are divided as to how she should behave. Elizabeth feels that a relationship should develop naturally and that the man will soon recognise the woman's sincere feelings. Charlotte is more hard-headed and worldly, feeling that the woman should be more assertive lest the chance of a financially attractive marriage be lost. In any case, she argues, however well a couple know each other in courtship, whether they will be happy in marriage is 'a matter of chance'. Unsuspecting the future turn of events, Elizabeth laughs that Charlotte herself would never act according to these principles.

Charlotte's words
remind us of the
novel's opening
sentence and her
future marriage to
Mr Collins.

Meanwhile, Darcy finds himself attracted to Elizabeth, less by her moderate beauty than by her liveliness and expressive dark eyes. Her particular charms are illustrated as she plays and sings to the company. She is less technically accomplished than her sister, Mary, but her performance is much more natural and pleasurable.

Elizabeth's spirited refusal serves only to enhance her attractiveness in Darcy's eyes.

Elizabeth is taken aback at Darcy's request to dance with her (all the more surprising, given his general distaste for the practice) and is 'determined' to decline the offer, believing him to be acting only out of formal politeness. To Miss Bingley's astonishment, Darcy confesses his interest in Elizabeth. She displays immediate signs of jealousy in her sarcastic jibe about the possibility of Mrs Bennet as mother-in-law.

COMMENT

The famous opening sentence introduces us to the main subject of the novel in an amusing and **ironic** (see Literary Terms) way. The opening words, 'It is a truth universally acknowledged', sound like the introduction to some grand philosophical insight but the sentence goes on to deliver what seems like a ridiculous **anticlimax** (see Literary Terms). What of love, we may ask? What of the single man's feelings? The irony is that in reality, the statement is nearer to the mark than we might care to admit, even today!

The opening statement is immediately dramatised in the conversation between Mr and Mrs Bennet.

Darcy's infamous pride emerges at the assembly. It colours Elizabeth's outlook until the truth begins to emerge in his letter (Chapters 35–6). Darcy later attributes his behaviour to shyness but his contempt for narrow country society is expressed elsewhere. At the same time, Darcy's manner sparks off an instinctive prejudice against one who is rich, powerful and can come and go as he pleases.

Darcy's cool aloofness is precisely what makes him fascinating.

Throughout the novel, Jane is presented as naively and unrealistically prejudiced in people's favour. However, her readiness to admit the possibility that Darcy is shy in strange company, shows her, on this occasion, to be more dispassionate than Elizabeth and less prone to jump to easy conclusions. How people are to be judged is a recurrent theme in the novel and at moments such as this, Jane Austen makes clear that no-one has a monopoly of insight.

GLOSSARY

Chapter 1
chaise and four a kind of carriage which shows that Bingley is well-off

Chapter 2
the assemblies dances open to the public
waited on visited

Chapter 6
impertinent intrusive, meddling
Vingt-un / Commerce popular card games
complacency (also **complacent**) pleased (The word at this time did not have the connotations of smugness it has today)

CHAPTERS 7–12

We learn more about Mr Bennet's circumstances and the fact that his estate and its income will pass to a distant relative. Mrs Bennet's inheritance is insufficient to support the daughters.

Militia were garrisoned throughout England as a defence against invasion by Napoleon.

The two youngest daughters, Catherine (Kitty) and Lydia, on one of their regular visits to their aunt, Mrs Phillips, in nearby Meryton learn that an army regiment has set up camp nearby. They return home thrilled at the prospect of officers in their finest uniforms. Mr Bennet comments dryly on his daughters' silliness but Mrs Bennet, ever alert to the possibility of glamorous suitors, shares their enthusiasm.

The excitement is interrupted by a message from Caroline Bingley inviting Jane to dine at Netherfield.

A STAY AT NETHERFIELD

Mrs Bennet is insistent that Jane should go on horseback, in the expectation that the onset of rain will enforce an overnight stay. News comes that, not only did the rain prevent Jane's immediate return, but that she has fallen ill as a result of being soaked. Mrs Bennet is delighted at the prospect of an even longer stay at Netherfield. Concerned for her sister's health, Elizabeth makes her way to Netherfield across muddy fields, whilst Catherine and Lydia set off in search of officers. Bingley's sisters are contemptuous of Elizabeth's bedraggled state but Darcy quietly admires her fresh and healthy complexion. Jane's condition is felt to be sufficiently serious for Elizabeth to be invited to stay the night.

Elizabeth is prepared to be unconventional and unladylike for the sake of her sister.

Elizabeth senses that it is only Bingley who shows any true concern for Jane. His sisters, especially Caroline, are more concerned with impressing Mr Darcy. When she is upstairs tending Jane, they criticise her appearance, condemn her behaviour and are scornful of her family's low status and connections with trade. Darcy, however, confesses that he found Elizabeth's eyes even more attractive after her walk but concedes that the Bennet sisters' background is a significant handicap in marriage.

The Bingley sisters conveniently forget that their inherited fortune was made through trade.

The evening is spent in a game of cards, which Elizabeth declines to join. Bingley goes out of his way to be kind to Elizabeth, while Miss Bingley continues to search for ways in which to embarrass or shame her. Elizabeth, however, is well able to hold her own and demonstrates her strength of mind and playful **wit** (see Literary Terms) when she enters into a spirited conversation about what constitutes an accomplished woman. Miss Bingley suggests to Darcy that Elizabeth's modesty about her own skills is a cunning way of inviting praise. Darcy's reply, condemning deceit, seems directed more at Miss

For Darcy, being an accomplished woman involves more than conventional domestic skills.

Bingley than Elizabeth. We learn that Jane is worse.

Mrs Bennet, accompanied by Catherine and Lydia, visits Jane, satisfies herself that the patient is not in danger, and then declares that she is far too ill to be moved. Mrs Bennet's rude and ignorant attempts at conversation are an embarrassment to everyone. She is uncivil to Darcy, and Elizabeth's attempts to change the subject lead only to Mrs Bennet's openly criticising Charlotte Lucas, whom she imagines to be a rival for Bingley's affections. Mrs Bennet's outburst is received in polite silence and Elizabeth is fearful lest her mother should compromise herself further. However, she soon leaves, but not before Lydia brazenly reminds Bingley of his proposal to mount a ball, a promise he agrees to keep.

Lydia is described as an attractive and fun-loving teenager.

Left alone to talk of the morning's events, Mr Darcy refuses to agree with Miss Bingley's remarks about Elizabeth, despite her mother's appalling behaviour.

The evening proceeds quietly. Miss Bingley attaches herself to Darcy who is attempting to write a letter to his sister. To his irritation, she interrupts him with flattery at every turn. Eventually, the conversation opens up into a discussion of Bingley's impulsive and impressionable character. Elizabeth joins in and once again shows her spirit and quickness of thought. Unlike Darcy and Elizabeth, Bingley does not enjoy the cut and thrust of lively debate and brings the conversation to an end with a rough joke at Darcy's expense. Elizabeth realises that Darcy is 'rather offended' and tactfully smooths over an awkward moment.

We gain some insight into Mr Darcy's knowledge of Bingley's character and his influence over him.

As Bingley's sisters play and sing at the piano, Elizabeth becomes aware of Darcy's gaze. The notion that she may be the object of his admiration crosses her mind, only to be dismissed immediately. She is taken

A STAY AT NETHERFIELD

back by his unexpected request for a dance. Believing him to be condescending and patronising, given his expressed distaste of dancing and of country living, she rejects his invitation with some force. She is surprised to note that Darcy displays no offence. In fact, he is so entranced by Elizabeth that he feels his only defence against her charms is the difference in their social rank.

Miss Bingley becomes increasingly jealous and tries to taunt Darcy with images of a demeaning future alliance with the Bennet family. Darcy refuses to rise to Caroline's bait but feels the Bingley sisters' rudeness when, during a walk in the grounds, they turn on to a path which is too narrow to allow Elizabeth to walk beside them.

Bingley's sisters are in good spirits because of the prospect of Jane's and Elizabeth's departure.

Jane, restored to health, joins the ladies, who engage her in warm and agreeable conversation. However, as soon as the gentlemen enter, Caroline has eyes only for Darcy, while Bingley devotes all his attention to Jane, much to Elizabeth's approval. After tea, Miss Bingley, obviously bored, tries to distract Darcy from his reading but he makes no response until Elizabeth agrees to accompany Caroline on a walk about the room, at which point he looks up for the first time.

Darcy declines to join them and in the ensuing conversation Elizabeth teases him into admitting his dislike of being an object of fun. He claims it as a matter of pride that he has rid himself of any characteristic that may incur ridicule. Amused at his earnestness and self-regard, she further goads him into confessing that his character is too intolerant and unforgiving. He breaks off the conversation, smiling at Elizabeth's readiness to oppose him in argument, and is left wondering whether he is becoming too attracted to her.

The time has come for Jane and Elizabeth to leave, much to Darcy's relief, as he is becoming seriously concerned about the warmth of his feelings towards Elizabeth. During the remainder of the stay, they barely speak to one another. Jane's return is far too soon for her mother, but Mr Bennet is quietly glad to see his two elder daughters at home. Mary is deep in her musical studies and as for Catherine and Lydia, their heads are full of regimental nonsense.

COMMENT   The episode at Netherfield is particularly important as it establishes the counteracting factors that draw Elizabeth and Darcy together and force them apart.

Elizabeth's three conversational encounters with Darcy, in which she is moved to provoke, tease and argue with him as an intellectual equal, suggest that her professed dislike is really unconscious fascination. Meanwhile, Darcy is becoming expressly attracted by Elizabeth's independent spirit and 'fine eyes'.

However, Miss Bingley's obvious jealousy of Elizabeth and Darcy's awareness of Elizabeth's social inferiority, accentuated by Mrs Bennet's vulgarity, are to prove major obstacles.

GLOSSARY   *Chapter 7*
sensible aware of
regimentals military uniform

Chapter 8
loo popular card game
comprehend include

Chapter 10
piquet popular card game
blots smudges by using too much ink

TEST YOURSELF (Chapters 1–12)

 A *Identify the person 'to whom' this comment refers.*

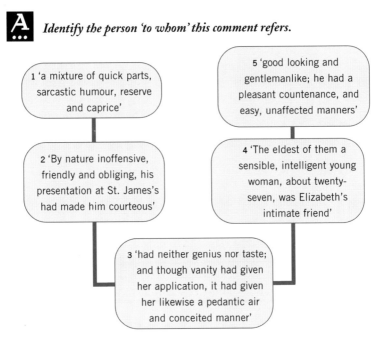

1 'a mixture of quick parts, sarcastic humour, reserve and caprice'

5 'good looking and gentlemanlike; he had a pleasant countenance, and easy, unaffected manners'

2 'By nature inoffensive, friendly and obliging, his presentation at St. James's had made him courteous'

4 'The eldest of them a sensible, intelligent young woman, about twenty-seven, was Elizabeth's intimate friend'

3 'had neither genius nor taste; and though vanity had given her application, it had given her likewise a pedantic air and conceited manner'

Check your answers on page 96.

B *Consider these issues.*

a What the novel's opening sentence suggests about attitudes to marriage.

b How Mr Bennet mocks and teases his wife.

c How Mrs Bennet's 'mean understanding, little information, and uncertain temper' (p. 7) are reflected in the way she speaks and behaves.

d The reasons why people regard Darcy as proud.

e How far Charlotte's opinions on how a woman should behave are justified.

f Mr Darcy's first impressions of Elizabeth.

g Elizabeth's first impressions of Darcy.

h The importance of the Netherfield episode to our understanding of some of the main characters.

CHAPTERS 13–14

The author enables us to 'observe' Mr Collins before she describes him directly.

At breakfast the following morning, Mr Bennet produces a letter from a distant cousin, Mr Collins, who according to the conditions of the entail, will inherit Longbourn estate. Having proudly declared himself a clergyman enjoying the patronage of Lady Catherine de Bourgh he announces his arrival at Longbourn that very day, Monday November 18th, and his intention to stay until the following Saturday. He claims his purpose is to make peace with the Bennet family and there is a hint that he might 'make every possible amends' for any injustice by marrying one of the daughters.

Mr Collins's letter is totally self-regarding and tactless.

Mrs Bennet's initial dismay at the prospect of meeting the 'odious' man who will rob the children of their inheritance is soon dispelled at the thought of a possible marriage. Elizabeth, however, is astonished at the pomposity of the letter and its mixture of 'servility and self-importance', a view that is confirmed on his arrival. At dinner that evening, he vulgarly talks of how Mrs Bennet's daughters should be 'well disposed of in marriage' and apologises at excessive length for suggesting that one of them might have performed the role of cook.

Mr Collins bathes in the reflected glory of Lady Catherine.

As the evening progresses Mr Collins proves to be an entirely ridiculous figure. His gratitude to Lady Catherine is unrestrained and he even reveals that it was she who suggested that he should marry. He is also wholly complimentary about Lady Catherine's daughter, Miss de Bourgh, who we learn later in the novel, is intended to marry Mr Darcy. However, although he describes her as 'charming … born to be a duchess', Mr Collins cannot disguise the fact that she is an unattractive, sickly girl of little accomplishment.

MR COLLINS ENTERS

Despite his disgust at frivolous fiction, Mr Collins is more interested in backgammon than Fordyce's Sermons.

Mr Bennet is highly amused at Mr Collins's pomposity and 'feeds' his visitor the chance to display his self-importance. His solemn sense of superiority is further emphasised when he proclaims surprise that young ladies such as Lydia should prefer works of fiction to morally improving sermons. He spends the remainder of the evening playing backgammon.

C OMMENT

Once encountered, it is impossible to forget Mr Collins. Jane Austen's skill in presenting this absurd character has much to do with her ability to make him all of a piece. He is entirely predictable; everything he says or does, down to the last detail, reinforces the picture of smug pomposity combined with cloying servility. The way he speaks is indistinguishable from the way he writes in its cumbersome expression and its utter insensitivity.

GLOSSARY

Chapter 13
preferred granted a parish; given a post as a clergyman

CHAPTERS 15–17

We are told of Mr Collins's background. We learn that for all his self-proclaimed pride in his own virtues and his readiness to be associated with aristocracy, he came from a narrow background, was lazy at university and extremely lucky to gain the prosperous living at Hunsford. As an eligible bachelor and convinced of his generosity towards the Bennet family, he has come to Longbourn to marry one of the daughters. His first choice is the most obviously beautiful daughter, Jane, but on learning from Mrs Bennet of her likely engagement, he immediately switches his attention to Elizabeth. Mrs Bennet is predictably delighted at the thought of shortly having two married daughters.

Ironically, Mr Collins is in a way 'a single man in possession of a good fortune'.

Mr Bennet, irritated that the privacy of his library should be invaded by Mr Collins, who is not the least interested in reading, recommends that he should accompany the sisters on a walk to Meryton.

Wickham immediately creates a favourable impression on all the sisters, including Elizabeth.

When they arrive, the sisters are introduced by an officer acquaintance of Kitty and Lydia to a handsome and charming stranger, Mr Wickham. At that moment, Bingley and Darcy arrive on horseback and, seeing the sisters, promptly make towards the company assembled in the street. Elizabeth is startled and overcome with curiosity when she notices that Darcy and Wickham are clearly surprised and deeply embarrassed to encounter each other.

The sisters and Mr Collins progress to their aunt's. Mrs Philips and Mr Collins indulge in exchanging exaggerated civilities. An invitation is extended to dine at the Philips' that evening with the possibility of Mr Wickham being in attendance.

When they return in the evening, accompanied by Mr Collins, the girls are delighted to hear that Mr Wickham has accepted Mr Philips' invitation to dinner. Settled in his place, Mr Collins continues to flatter Mrs Philips by comparing her drawing room favourably with Lady Catherine's *small summer* breakfast parlour. The

WICKHAM ENTERS ELIZABETH'S LIFE AND REVEALS SOME SECRETS

The vastly expensive fireplace to which Mr Collins refers suggests Lady Catherine's vulgar pleasure in conspicuous wealth.

girls' boredom at hearing Mr Collins's catalogue the wonders of Lady Catherine's mansion is relieved with the appearance of Wickham and the other gentlemen.

The normally level-headed Elizabeth is immediately won over by Wickham's easy, out-going manner and his charming conversation. Elizabeth's curiosity about the relationship between Wickham and Darcy is soon answered. Unprompted, Wickham enquires after Darcy's whereabouts, plans and Elizabeth's acquaintance with him. Elizabeth readily expresses her dislike of Darcy and Wickham appears to take her into his confidence by giving an account of his past history. Wickham's father had been a loyal employee of Darcy's father who in turn had taken the young Wickham under his wing. He had promised Wickham a career in the church with the certainty of the appointment to a desirable living. Mr Darcy, however, had gone back on his father's promise and given the living to another. Elizabeth is shocked at such an injustice but impressed when Wickham declares that he can never expose Darcy out of respect for his father. Even so, she cannot understand how Darcy could have acted so heartlessly. Wickham's explanation is that Darcy is jealous of his late father's affection for Wickham and has come to thoroughly dislike him as a result. Wickham agrees with Elizabeth that Darcy is motivated by pride and goes on to suggest that his generosity and good deeds stem from excessive pride in his reputation rather than from sincere concern for others. His treatment of Wickham, however, is a result of even 'stronger impulses'.

Elizabeth is taken in by Wickham's sorry tale.

When Elizabeth wonders how such an amiable person as Bingley could enjoy the company of such a disagreeable man as Darcy, Wickham replies that Darcy can be pleasant when it suits him. Overhearing mention

Elizabeth is prepared to believe Wickham's account because it reinforces her prejudices about Darcy.

of Lady Catherine de Bourgh, Wickham explains to Elizabeth that she is Mr Darcy's aunt and that Miss de Bourgh and Darcy are believed to be due to marry. Elizabeth is amused at the thought of Miss Bingley's designs on Darcy being thwarted and she is pleased that Wickham is able to confirm her view that Lady Catherine must be an arrogant woman.

As Elizabeth returns home her head is full of thoughts of Wickham and his revelations.

Elizabeth and Jane present their conflicting 'prejudices' about Wickham and Darcy.

The next day Elizabeth tells Jane about what she has learned. Characteristically, Jane refuses to attribute blame to either Darcy or Wickham, although privately she is concerned whether Bingley really has been used by Darcy. Elizabeth is convinced that Wickham was telling the truth.

An invitation to the planned ball at Netherfield arrives which moves Elizabeth to dream of dancing with Wickham. Unfortunately, out of politeness, she is obliged to agree to Mr Collins's offer to share the first two dances. In fact, she comes to realise that Mr Collins has chosen her to be his wife but she ignores her mother's support for the idea. The week drags. The rain prevents any excursions to Meryton. Only the prospect of the ball offers the girls any relief.

COMMENT   Wickham is to all appearances everything that Mr Collins is not: handsome, charming, well-spoken and approachable. The **irony** (see Literary Terms) is that they are both equally lacking in moral scruples, both wholly mercenary and both prepared to exploit women. Wickham, however, has more in common with the totally immoral, sweet talking villains of **romantic fiction** (see Literary Terms).

Elizabeth's curiosity and eagerness to soak up any scandal concerning the 'hate figure' Darcy, causes her to

WICKHAM ENTERS ELIZABETH'S LIFE AND REVEALS SOME SECRETS

overlook Wickham's overfamiliarity and lack of propriety. She is also prepared to excuse Wickham's absence (see Chapter 18) from the one ball she had been looking forward to as evidence of his tact, rather than as deliberate avoidance of Darcy. She later appreciates Darcy's sense of honour and discretion in not talking freely about Wickham.

GLOSSARY

Chapter 15

living the property and income which were given to the chosen clergyman

CHAPTER 18

Once again Charlotte shows her unsentimental approach where matters of feeling and wealth are concerned.

At the Netherfield ball Elizabeth is disappointed from the outset; she searches in vain for Wickham, only to be told that he is absent. She suspects Darcy to be responsible. She is surprised and irritated when she finds herself accepting Darcy's offer of a dance. Charlotte Lucas warns her not to allow her liking for Wickham to offend a man of such importance as Mr Darcy. As they dance, Elizabeth tries unsuccessfully to probe Darcy concerning Wickham. Darcy becomes distant when she raises the matter and although he is impeccably polite, it is clear that he wishes to change the subject. Elizabeth can only believe that Wickham was telling the truth but not before she and Darcy have had a lively conversation which touches on the mysteries of Darcy's character. Furthermore, she considers Miss Bingley's warning not to believe Wickham as 'impudent' and she even discounts Jane's assurances of Bingley's trust in Darcy's integrity. For his part, Darcy privately forgives Elizabeth but feels nothing but anger towards Wickham.

Despite herself, Elizabeth still cannot avoid being stimulated by her conversations with Mr Darcy.

The remainder of the evening proves a protracted source of shame for Elizabeth as she is forced to witness

Elizabeth is shamed five times in succession.

the embarrassing behaviour of members of her family. First, Mr Collins, ignoring Elizabeth's protestations and oblivious of etiquette, forces his fawning attentions on Mr Darcy who receives him with polite astonishment. Secondly, her mother talks brazenly to Lady Lucas about her confidence in the impending marriage of Jane to Mr Bingley and loudly disparages Mr Darcy, all within his earshot. Elizabeth is convinced that he has been listening. Thirdly, Mary's attempts at entertaining the company in song are so feeble as to find Elizabeth 'in agonies'. Then, to the amazement of half the room, Mr Collins loudly delivers a speech on his duties as a clergyman, the first of which he declares, is to secure his personal income. Finally, Mrs Bennet contrives to be the last to leave and Elizabeth has to endure the embarrassed silence in which her mother's chatter and Mr Collins's speeches were received.

COMMENT

The behaviour of members of Elizabeth's family at the Netherfield ball displays a crassness and lack of refinement that only serves to feed Darcy's sense of their inferiority. Elizabeth is embarrassed because her own sense of decency and decorum is offended, but the scene also foreshadows her later shame at her family's even more serious deficiencies and her despair at what she thinks must be Darcy's justifiable reactions.

CHAPTERS 19–23

As time is short before his return to Hunsford Parsonage, Mr Collins decides to propose. Mrs Bennet readily agrees to his request for an audience with her daughter and excitedly scurries upstairs leaving Elizabeth to face Mr Collins.

Even by the conventions of the day, his proposal is excessively formal and consists entirely of reasons why *he* should marry. He makes clear that he is bestowing

MR COLLINS TRIES AND TRIES AGAIN

Mr Collins claims an honour on the Bennet household. When Elizabeth
to be 'indifferent refuses him with all the civility she can summon, Mr
to fortune' but he Collins flatters himself that she is merely being coy.
is well aware of Her continued resistance fails to shake his conviction
Elizabeth's meagre that she will eventually accept, although he does warn
inheritance. her that she may not receive another such an offer of
marriage. Eventually, Elizabeth leaves it to her father to
convince Mr Collins that she really does not want to
marry him.

Unlike Charlotte, Mrs Bennet is distressed on hearing of Elizabeth's
Elizabeth is refusal but reassures Mr Collins that Mr Bennet will
prepared to risk talk her round. Mr Bennet, however, derives wry
remaining amusement from the situation and refuses to intervene.
unmarried. After much distracted pleading and cajoling on Mrs
Bennet's part, which Elizabeth rather enjoys rebutting,
Mr Collins withdraws his offer as ponderously and
wordily as he had made it. Significantly, Charlotte
Lucas has entered and is the subject of Mr Collins's
close attention.

In the aftermath of Elizabeth's refusal, Mrs Bennet's
continues to be bad-tempered while Mr Collins
maintains a 'resentful silence' towards Elizabeth.
He shows no lack of lengthy civility to Charlotte,
however.

Elizabeth meets Wickham once more in Meryton and
admires his tact when he explains that he chose to stay
away from the ball in order to avoid Darcy. She is
flattered when Wickham and an officer friend
accompany the sisters home.

Jane's agony When they arrive home, Jane receives a letter from
begins. Miss Bingley announcing their sudden return to
London. Jane is naturally distressed and particularly
hurt by Miss Bingley's suggestion that Darcy's sister,
Georgiana, is a fine prospect for the hand of Bingley.
Elizabeth, however, is confident of Bingley's

Elizabeth forgets or does not appreciate how easily Bingley is influenced.

attachment to Jane and attributes his sister's suggestions to malice and wishful thinking. Jane cannot accept that Caroline could be so devious and, despite Elizabeth's reassurances concerning his independent spirit, despairs of Bingley's early return.

Elizabeth feels let down by Charlotte.

Elizabeth is grateful that Charlotte has taken on the burden of entertaining Mr Collins but cannot suspect that her friend is hopeful that he will propose to her. Before long he does just that and she readily accepts. She is under no illusions concerning Mr Collins's character but the prospect of financial security outweighs any thoughts of romance or affection. Elizabeth is shocked and disappointed when Charlotte breaks the news to her in private, feeling that her friend has disgraced herself.

The Bennet family's reaction to the news of Charlotte's engagement neatly reflects their various characters.

When Sir William tells the rest of the Bennet family of the engagement, they react in predictable ways. When the truth has sunk in, Mrs Bennet becomes entirely distracted and blames Elizabeth for ruining her chances of marrying off one of her daughters. Mr Bennet derives perverse satisfaction from the thought he is not uniquely blessed with the company of foolish women. Jane is surprised but wishes the couple happiness. Elizabeth feels that a barrier has come between herself and her friend and is drawn closer to her elder sister. For Kitty and Lydia the news is merely a subject for gossip as Mr Collins is 'merely a clergyman'.

Meanwhile, Jane has been awaiting news of the Bingleys but as the days pass the two sisters become more anxious especially as there is a rumour that Bingley will not return that winter. Even Elizabeth's trust in Bingley's determination begins to weaken and she wonders whether he has been influenced by his sisters and Darcy.

MR COLLINS TRIES AND TRIES AGAIN

Mrs Bennet's misery is compounded by the thought that Charlotte will one day supplant her as mistress of Longbourn.

COMMENT   Charlotte's engagement sets the seal on one important view of marriage. Elizabeth is shocked and disappointed for reasons of integrity. Mrs Bennet is shocked, disappointed and full of recrimination because a golden opportunity has slipped through their fingers. The Lucases see the engagement as a coup. For the moment, the sentiment of the novel's opening sentence seems amply justified.

GLOSSARY   *Chapter 19*
4 per cents government investments which offered a four percent rate of interest

Chapter 21
hot pressed paper a very expensive kind of writing paper
two full courses a 'course' at this time consisted of a (sometimes quite large) number of dishes set out at once, not served separately as today

Chapter 22
coming out the name given to the formal series of events which a young woman attended to mark her entry into adult society

TEST YOURSELF (Chapters 13–23)

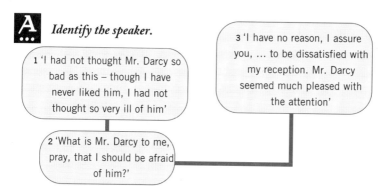

A *Identify the speaker.*

1 'I had not thought Mr. Darcy so bad as this – though I have never liked him, I had not thought so very ill of him'

2 'What is Mr. Darcy to me, pray, that I should be afraid of him?'

3 'I have no reason, I assure you, ... to be dissatisfied with my reception. Mr. Darcy seemed much pleased with the attention'

Identify the person 'to whom' this comment refers.

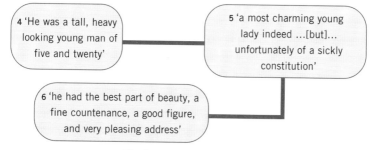

4 'He was a tall, heavy looking young man of five and twenty'

5 'a most charming young lady indeed ...[but]... unfortunately of a sickly constitution'

6 'he had the best part of beauty, a fine countenance, a good figure, and very pleasing address'

Check your answers on page 96.

B *Consider these issues.*

a Why Mr Collins's letter prompts Elizabeth to ask 'Can he be a sensible man, Sir?'

b How Mr Collins depicts Lady Catherine.

c Why Wickham is able to make such a favourable impression on Elizabeth.

d What Wickham's openness and Darcy's reticence about their previous connection suggest about their respective characters.

e How members of the Bennet family disgrace themselves at the Netherfield ball.

f The skill with which Jane Austen constructs Mr Collins's proposal so as to match his character.

g How Jane and Elizabeth assess Caroline Bingley's character and motives.

h Whether Charlotte is right to accept Mr Collins's proposal.

CHAPTERS 24–7

Jane receives confirmation from Miss Bingley that they intend to remain in London for the winter. Jane cannot but feel that her relationship with Bingley is at an end, especially as Caroline stresses his affection for Miss Darcy, but she resigns herself to the situation with her usual serenity. Elizabeth is more critical, suspecting that her sister's happiness has been ruined by the influences of the Bingley sisters and Darcy. Jane is ready to see the best in everyone, even those who have been the cause of hurt, but Elizabeth has come to take a more jaundiced view of human character as she continues to be astonished at Charlotte's engagement to 'a conceited, pompous, narrow-minded, silly man'.

Mr Bennet cannot be aware of the irony of his joke about Wickham.

With his usual tongue-in-cheek cynicism, Mr Bennet sees that at least Jane has achieved an enviable status for having been crossed in love. Furthermore, he suggests that Elizabeth should emulate her sister by encouraging Wickham, who would jilt her 'creditably'. By this time Wickham has become generally accepted as one who has suffered at Mr Darcy's hands. **Ironically** (see Literary Terms), only Jane considers that there may be another side to the story.

Mrs Gardiner is thoughtful and sympathetic.

Mrs Bennet's brother and sister-in-law, the Gardiners, come to stay. They are a pleasant and sensible couple and Mrs Gardiner is a particular favourite of Jane and Elizabeth. On the subject of Jane's disappointment, she is somewhat dubious of the true sincerity of Bingley's passions but sympathises with the hurt that Jane must feel. Elizabeth is delighted when Jane is invited to stay with the Gardiners in London and secretly harbours the slim hope Bingley might yet find Jane's nearness impossible to resist.

When Mrs Gardiner meets Wickham she feels some disquiet at his intimacy with Elizabeth but enjoys

Mrs Gardner's good sense is revealed in her reluctance to form hasty judgements and in her advice to Elizabeth concerning Wickham.

talking to him about Pemberley and Mr Darcy's father. By way of confirming the general opinion of Mr Darcy, she dimly remembers him being reported as 'a very proud, ill-natured boy'.

Mrs Gardiner warns Elizabeth about becoming too attracted to Wickham. He is good company but has no fortune. Elizabeth reassures her aunt that although she is much taken by him, she is not in love but that she cannot be entirely responsible for how her feelings may develop.

Mr Collins and Charlotte are married. Elizabeth promises to visit Charlotte in Kent but feels that their friendship will never be quite the same again.

Caroline Bingley's true colours are revealed.

Jane writes that she has paid an all too brief visit to Caroline Bingley but that she expects an early return visit. A month passes before Caroline comes to see Jane. Caroline's offhand behaviour finally leads Jane reluctantly to acknowledge that Elizabeth was right about Caroline's deceitful character.

Meanwhile, Wickham has turned his attentions on a certain Miss King, a wealthy young heiress. Elizabeth convinces herself that she feels no disappointment and accepts Wickham's desire for financial security.

It is March and Elizabeth, accompanied by Sir William Lucas and his daughter Maria, sets out on the promised visit to Charlotte in Kent. She breaks her journey at the Gardiners' in London. Mrs Gardiner questions Wickham's motives for his sudden interest in Miss King. Elizabeth defends him against the charge of being mercenary but cannot avoid sounding generally depressed and disillusioned. In order to raise her niece's spirits, the Gardiners propose she join them on an extensive tour of England that summer.

Elizabeth becomes dispirited.

COMMENT   Elizabeth shows a keener awareness of people's motives than Jane but accepts Wickham at face value.

JANE'S DISAPPOINTMENT

The less sympathetic side to Mr Bennet begins to emerge.

GLOSSARY

Chapter 24
temper personality, outlook on life

Chapter 26
discover reveal, make him aware

CHAPTERS 28–29

Much cheered by seeing her sister and the Gardiners' invitation, Elizabeth continues her journey to Hunsford. On her arrival, Mr Collins is soon showing off the comforts and delights of the parsonage. Elizabeth senses he is pointedly trying to make her regret the 'sacrifice' she made in refusing his proposal. Charlotte appears entirely contented with her new home. The next morning Elizabeth is called to the window to witness Miss de Bourgh sitting in her carriage talking to Charlotte. She deplores her rudeness in keeping Charlotte standing outside in the cold March winds but takes a mischievous delight in the thought that Darcy is destined to marry such an ill-tempered, sickly creature.

Even though she 'hates' him Elizabeth is drawn into thinking of Darcy.

Mr Collins conducted tour reminds us of an overenthusiastic estate agent!

The next day the whole party dines at Rosings. Mr Collins is duly extravagant in his praise of the wonders of what they are about to experience and as they approach the house, Sir William and his daughter are visibly in awe of the scene. Elizabeth, however, is entirely at ease. She is soon able to observe Lady Catherine soaking up endless compliments from Mr Collins and Sir William and behaving in as arrogant, patronising and dictatorial manner as she had imagined. Elizabeth feels particularly insulted by Lady Catherine's impertinent questions about her family but she manages to remain polite. At one point, however, Elizabeth bridles at being rudely asked her age. Lady Catherine's evident surprise at her refusal to give a direct reply, prompts Elizabeth to speculate that she may be the first person to stand up to her Ladyship.

COMMENT   Elizabeth's readiness to resist Lady Catherine's overbearing manner anticipates later developments.

Lady Catherine's close questioning of Elizabeth about her family shows her impertinence and readiness to interfere in other's affairs.

CHAPTERS 30–33

The days pass routinely. Elizabeth appreciates how Charlotte has organised her living arrangements to avoid continuous contact with her husband and she sees that Lady Catherine's officiousness extends to interfering in the lives of the local villagers and tenants.

Darcy's early visit to the parsonage with Colonel Fitzwilliam, hints at his continuing interest in Elizabeth.

News comes that Mr Darcy and his cousin, Colonel Fitzwilliam, are to visit their aunt at Rosings. Despite her feelings towards Darcy, Elizabeth welcomes the prospect of new company. The gentlemen pay a surprisingly early courtesy call on the Collins which Charlotte believes is entirely due to Elizabeth's presence. Darcy says little but appears confused when Elizabeth mentions that Jane is in London.

Under the cover of a formal conversation, Darcy tries to confess something of his true character.

Now that Darcy and Colonel Fitzwilliam are staying at Rosings, invitations to dinner become less frequent. However, when the occasion does arise, Elizabeth is charmed by Colonel Fitzwilliam and Darcy is quick to observe their warm conversation. Lady Catherine dominates proceedings as usual and her patronising attitude towards Elizabeth embarrasses Darcy. When Elizabeth begins to sing, Darcy moves over to the piano so that he can observe her more closely. A lively conversation ensues in which Elizabeth provocatively charges Darcy with being an unsociable person, to which he replies that he is always shy in strange company.

The next morning, Elizabeth, sitting alone in the parsonage, is surprised by the sudden appearance of Mr Darcy. They engage in a strained conversation and Darcy will not be drawn on the subject of Bingley's rapid departure from Netherfield. At one point, however, he appears to suggest surprise that Elizabeth could possibly be satisfied with such a narrow society as offered by Longbourn.

Charlotte may be safe and dull but she is perceptive.

When Charlotte returns she is tempted to believe that Darcy is falling in love with Elizabeth. Elizabeth dismisses the idea but Charlotte continues to wonder at the frequency of the two gentlemen's visits, for she has also noticed how Colonel Fitzwilliam and Elizabeth enjoy each other's company. She has observed Darcy's admiring glances at Elizabeth and in her own mind, she decides that he would make the more desirable husband of the two.

Elizabeth is surprised at how frequently she and Darcy meet when she wanders along one of the estate's least frequented paths. Little is said during these encounters, although they leave Elizabeth feeling mildly irritated.

Colonel Fitzwilliam's revelations further fuels Elizabeth's resentment of Darcy.

On one occasion, however, she is surprised not by Darcy but by Colonel Fitzwilliam. When the conversation turns to Darcy and his influence over others, Elizabeth is shocked to learn that, as the Colonel understands it, Darcy intervened to rescue a friend from a 'most imprudent marriage'. Elizabeth is left feeling angry and indignant at Darcy, whose arrogance and pride have destroyed her sister's happiness. She also takes Darcy's actions as a personal slight because she suspects that he was influenced less by her mother's lack of social graces than by the Bennet family's lack of connections.

Comment   Lady Catherine's treatment of the local community
            contrasts sharply with Darcy's (see Chapter 43).

            Darcy's declarations about family and travel echo his
            earlier sentiments about rural society.

            In her own way, Lady Catherine proves as vulgar as
            Mrs Bennet.

chapters 34–38

Rereading Jane's letters, Elizabeth concludes that her
sister is truly depressed. Darcy enters and, after a few
polite enquires after her health, suddenly declares his
love and proposes marriage, making clear that his
passion has fought with his awareness of her social
inferiority.

Elizabeth's animosity towards Darcy is at its most intense.

Fuelled by what she has just learned from Colonel
Fitzwilliam, Elizabeth's reply is heated and straight-
talking. She regards his account of how he had
overcome his natural prejudice towards her social
position as 'uncivil'. She also accuses him of ruining her
sister's life and being the source of Wickham's
misfortunes. Darcy protests that he was merely being
frank and it would have been dishonest of him not to
admit his concerns about their respective social
standing.

Ironically, Elizabeth's stinging rejection of Darcy is the key factor that brings them together.

Elizabeth fiercely retorts that the manner of his
proposal was ungentlemanly and she proceeds to accuse
him of being arrogant, self-centred and uncaring of the
feelings of others. Darcy is hurt, politely wishes her well
and leaves. Elizabeth is left in a state of total
bewilderment. She is full of indignation at the man's
'abominable pride' but in a strange way she also feels
flattered that a man of Darcy's distinction should have
proposed to her.

Elizabeth's mixed feelings open the possibility of a change of heart.

Out for her walk the following day, Elizabeth cannot avoid Darcy who hands her a letter and promptly withdraws.

The letter is long and explains his actions concerning Bingley and Wickham. He makes no apology for 'detaching' Bingley from Jane. He explains that the difference in social station might have been bridged but her family's 'lack of propriety' could not be excused. Jane and Elizabeth, however, were excused this charge. Darcy also remarks that Jane's lack of any obvious outward response to Bingley's attentions, influenced his assessment of the affair. Darcy, however, does admit to a perhaps unworthy deception in concealing Jane's presence in London.

We are reminded of Charlotte's earlier comments on Jane's reluctance to show her feelings.

On the subject of Wickham, he accepts that Elizabeth could not possibly have guessed the truth. Wickham is a wastrel, who had given up any claim on the church living he had been promised, preferring to accept from Darcy three thousand pounds, on the pretext of studying for the law. When the money ran out, he returned to demand that Darcy present him with the living. When Darcy refused, Wickham showed nothing but resentment. Worst of all, Wickham tried to seduce and elope with Darcy's sister; she was just fifteen. His motive could only have been revenge and the attractions of Miss Darcy's thirty thousand pounds. Darcy ends by recommending Elizabeth to Colonel Fitzwilliam if confirmation of these details were needed.

Elizabeth begins to reconsider.

Elizabeth's first reaction is to reject Darcy's account out of hand. His attitude toward Jane is insulting and confirms his arrogance, whilst the account of Wickham's character produces nothing but feelings of horror. On reflection, however, she begins to realise how prejudiced and self-deluding she has been. She wonders how she could possibly have overlooked Wickham's indiscretion in talking as he did at their first meeting. Casting her mind back, she realises that nothing was known about Wickham and there is no evidence to support the high opinion in which he is held. She now appreciates his cowardice in avoiding Darcy by not attending the Netherfield ball and in criticising him publicly when he had left the district.

Elizabeth's rationality begins to overcome her prejudice.

She cannot blame Darcy for his impressions of her sister, which only confirm Charlotte's concern about Jane's failure to show her true feelings. Furthermore, she is painfully aware of her family's lack of breeding and can take little comfort from Darcy's compliments concerning Jane and herself.

The gentlemen have departed and despite Lady Catherine's protestations Elizabeth is planning to return home. In the remaining days, she gives much thought to Darcy's letter and her anger towards him begins to turn to respect. She cannot defend her family from his criticisms; 'they were hopeless of remedy'. Even her father cannot escape rebuke. He has failed to control the moody Catherine and the flirtatious Lydia, whose excesses have been encouraged by an irresponsible mother. Elizabeth cannot escape the truth that her family are responsible for Jane's misfortunes.

The mention of Catherine and Lydia prepares us for the next development in the story.

DARCY'S BOMBSHELL

Elizabeth takes her leave of Charlotte and Mr Collins and travels the short distance to London. Jane is to return with her to Longbourn. Elizabeth is left wondering when and how she is to tell Jane about Darcy's revelations.

COMMENT   These chapters record the first major turning point in the story as both Elizabeth and Darcy are forced to reassess their outlook.

Darcy's proposal could not be more unfortunately timed, so incensed is Elizabeth at what she believes is the ruin of Jane's chances of happiness. However, the **irony** (see Literary Terms) is that her intense anger prompts her to step beyond the bounds of etiquette (she is far more polite to the foolish Mr Collins) and accuse Darcy of ungentlemanly behaviour. We learn later that it was this charge that made Darcy re-examine his motives. Even so, in the midst of her indignation is the faintest hint of romantic stirring, when she briefly allows herself to feel flattered that one such as Darcy should have proposed to her.

Darcy's letter sets Elizabeth thinking. Her clear-sighted analysis of the letter confirms her intelligence and her willingness to see another's point of view. It also rather sets her somewhat apart from her family whom she loves but whose actions she cannot always justify.

Lady Catherine represents the old aristocracy at its worst: rich but devoid of taste; privileged but insolent; powerful but irresponsible. Lady Catherine has the social status but lacks the attendant values; Elizabeth lacks the status but displays a superior sense of values.

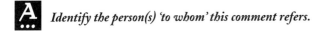TEST YOURSELF (Chapters 24–38)

A *Identify the person(s) 'to whom' this comment refers.*

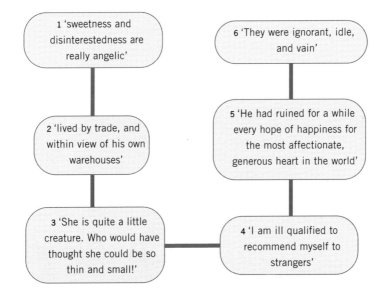

1 'sweetness and disinterestedness are really angelic'

6 'They were ignorant, idle, and vain'

2 'lived by trade, and within view of his own warehouses'

5 'He had ruined for a while every hope of happiness for the most affectionate, generous heart in the world'

3 'She is quite a little creature. Who would have thought she could be so thin and small!'

4 'I am ill qualified to recommend myself to strangers'

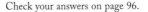

Check your answers on page 96.

B *Consider these issues.*

a Elizabeth's and Jane's assessment of Charlotte's marriage.

b The relationship between Elizabeth and her aunt, Mrs Gardiner.

c What Jane's letters reveal about her relationship with Miss Bingley.

d Our impressions of Mr and Mrs Collins at home.

e How Jane Austen builds up a picture of Lady Catherine's personality.

f How Darcy's admiration of Elizabeth is revealed in words and action *before* he proposes.

g Why Elizabeth refuses Darcy.

h How Darcy's letter forces Elizabeth to reconsider her attitudes.

ELIZABETH'S PROBLEM FAMILY

CHAPTERS 39–42

On the journey home, the two sisters stop at a coaching inn where they are met by Kitty and Lydia. The younger sisters have squandered all their money shopping but Lydia is in such good spirits that she offers to treat them all to a meal so long as Jane and Elizabeth pay! In the course of her ceaseless gossip about balls and officers, she announces that Wickham's regiment is about to remove to Brighton. She has been begging her father to take them all down to Brighton for the summer. She also reveals that the affair between Wickham and Miss King is over. Knowing what she does, Elizabeth even sympathises with Lydia's rather tasteless remarks on the subject.

Lydia's 'animal spirits' take on a new importance in the story.

When they have arrived home, Elizabeth declines Lydia's invitation to walk into Meryton, largely because she dreads meeting Wickham again. She takes comfort that he will soon be moving on to Brighton, only to learn that her mother has been nagging Mr Bennet to agree to Lydia's scheme.

Lydia is aided and abetted by her mother.

At last Elizabeth is able to tell Jane of those parts of Darcy's letter that deal with Wickham. She decides *not* to reveal Darcy's influence with Bingley. Jane finds it difficult to believe that Wickham could be so bad. Elizabeth cannot forgive herself for being so prejudiced towards Darcy, especially as she sees her dislike as stemming from pride in her own cleverness.

Elizabeth examines her own pride and prejudice.

The two sisters agree not to broadcast the truth about Wickham, Jane because she fears it will do him harm, Elizabeth because it was given to her in confidence. Elizabeth detects a sadness about Jane and realises that her feelings for Bingley have not weakened. She finds little to say in response to her mother's persistent questioning.

The sisters' decision not to reveal Wickham's true character has unforeseen consequences.

The Regiment have a mere week remaining in Meryton. When Lydia is invited to accompany Colonel Forster and his wife to Brighton her joy is uncontained. Elizabeth is acutely aware of the dangers in allowing her to go and appeals to her father to withhold his consent. She warns Mr Bennet that Lydia's behaviour has already brought the family into disrepute, Mr Bennet laughs off the suggestion. When Elizabeth presses him further by stressing Lydia's shallow and flirtatious nature, his response is that he finds it more convenient to grant Lydia's wishes, on the grounds that she can hardly become any worse, than to attempt to keep her under control.

Mr Bennet abdicates his responsibility.

Since she has returned to Longbourn, Elizabeth has been unable to avoid Wickham but now can see his charming manners in a different light: they now possess 'an affectation and a sameness to disgust and weary'. In their last conversation, Elizabeth is deliberately ambiguous about what she has learned from Colonel Fitzwilliam and Mr Darcy. Wickham's discomfiture makes it clear that he is worried that she knows the truth.

Elizabeth is able to interpret the 'evidence' of Wickham's conversation quite differently.

With Lydia's departure, Elizabeth is left to reflect on the deficiencies of her family and particularly on her father's weakness. Swayed by beauty and a superficially lively personality, he had married unwisely and before long all affection and respect had faded. His response to this failure was not to turn to gambling or to drink but to retreat to his study from where he could regard his family with the eye of an amused observer. Elizabeth is now acutely aware that her father's detached and cynical outlook amounts to irresponsibility towards his children. Their uncontrolled behaviour threatens the family's good name.

Mr Bennet's attitudes are explained.

Otherwise, she is bored and the tedium of life at Longbourn is only relieved by the prospect of the trip

ELIZABETH'S PROBLEM FAMILY

with the Gardiners. As the time approaches Mrs Gardiner writes to explain that the trip will have to be cut short so that they will not be able to journey further northwards than Derbyshire.

When the party eventually arrives in Derbyshire, Elizabeth is at first reluctant to visit Pemberley for fear of meeting Darcy. However, reassured by the chambermaid at a local inn that the family are not residence, her mind is put at ease.

C OMMENT   These chapters serve as an interlude between Elizabeth's last encounter with Darcy in Kent and their next encounter in Derbyshire. The fact that these emotionally significant events take place away from Longbourn emphasise the independence of Elizabeth's inner life. Her eventual move to become mistress of Pemberley reflects how she has outgrown the confines of Longbourn. It was Darcy who had earlier exclaimed '*You* cannot have been always at Longbourn' (p. 149). These chapters focus on some of the worst aspects of life at Longbourn.

GLOSSARY   *Chapter 39*
bandbox round box for a hat

Chapter 41
peculiar particular

CHAPTERS 43–45

Elizabeth sees a reflection of the owner in Pemberley's civilised appearance.

Pemberley is impressive. Elizabeth is 'delighted' with the grounds and admires the elegance of the rooms which she feels reflects the taste of their owner. She is even tempted to imagine what it would be like to be mistress of Pemberley. They are shown around by the housekeeper, an honest, plain-spoken woman who offers unqualified praise of Darcy's consideration and generosity. His reputation for being proud and aloof is simply owing to the fact that 'he does not rattle away like other young men'. Elizabeth is astonished at this side to Darcy's character, which seems so much at odds with her own understanding.

As Elizabeth and the Gardiners walk away from the house, Darcy suddenly appears; he has returned unexpectedly early. Shame and distress envelop Elizabeth as she cannot bear to think what Darcy will make of her presence at his home. To her amazement, Darcy conducts himself with impeccable civility and even enquires warmly about her family. After he has left, Elizabeth begins to regain her composure but her thoughts are constantly on Darcy and what he must be feeling about her.

A new side to Darcy's character is revealed for the first time.

Before long, Darcy reappears and joins them on their walk. He engages Mr and Mrs Gardiner in amiable conversation and Elizabeth takes pleasure in the fact that she has some relations of whom she need not feel ashamed. As Elizabeth listens to Darcy she is drawn to wonder whether he still loves her but she is still rather nervous of his presence.

Romantic thoughts begin to creep into Elizabeth's consciousness.

She is informed that Bingley and his sisters are due the next day but she is particularly intrigued and flattered when Darcy tells her that his sister wants to meet her.

ESCAPE TO PEMBERLEY

As they leave Pemberley, Mr and Mrs Gardiner, who know him only by reputation, try to weigh up Darcy's character. When Mrs Gardiner dwells on his supposed treatment of Wickham, Elizabeth rushes to Darcy's defence.

Almost as soon as she has arrived, Darcy brings his sister to meet Elizabeth. It turns out that the 'proud' Georgiana is merely extremely shy and Elizabeth is relieved that she is simply a pleasant, unassuming young woman. Bingley soon arrives and Elizabeth poses *As ever, Elizabeth* herself the problem of guessing the true feelings of her *is concerned for* visitors. She satisfies herself that Bingley shows no *Jane's happiness.* attachment to Miss Darcy and when he recalls the precise date he last saw Jane, she is gratified that his affection for her sister is undimmed. As for Darcy, she continues to be struck by his good humour and readiness to please. His manner is wholly different from that she had witnessed at Netherfield and Rosings.

Elizabeth tries to An invitation is extended to dine at Pemberley and *assess her true* when the visitors leave, Elizabeth hastens away to be *feelings.* alone. Her feelings towards Darcy have undergone a decisive change. She dismisses any thoughts of hatred. They have been supplanted by a warm sense of gratitude, respect and concern for his well-being. Nevertheless, she unsure whether she wants to reawaken thoughts of marriage.

Caroline Bingley's Elizabeth and the Gardiners visit Pemberley, where the *tactless remarks* party includes the Bingley sisters. The atmosphere is *contrast with the* rather strained at first and only eased by the cordial *civility of her* conversation of Mrs Gardiner and Miss Darcy's *'social inferiors'.* companion, Mrs Annesley. Miss Bingley cannot resist showing her jealousy of Elizabeth by making a thinly disguised reference to Wickham. Elizabeth feels for the embarrassment that Darcy and his sister must be feeling.

When Elizabeth and the Gardeners have left, Miss

Bingley sets about venting her bile by criticising Elizabeth's appearance in some detail. Eventually, Darcy's composure snaps and he leaves the room praising Elizabeth as one of the handsomest women he had ever met.

Darcy's passion is revealed.

COMMENT   The visit to Pemberley is crucial within the narrative scheme of the novel as, for the first time, we see Darcy relaxed and wholly at ease on his home ground. This previously unsuspected face of Darcy impresses the Gardiners and affects Elizabeth deeply.

There are subtler dimensions to the visit as well. It is not only Darcy's behaviour that moves Elizabeth but the *place* as well. She later confides to Jane that she first felt she loved Darcy when she saw 'his beautiful grounds at Pemberley' (p. 301). Jane Austen's description of the grounds stresses the effortless blend of art and nature: 'She had never seen a place for which nature had done more, or where natural beauty had been so little counteracted by an awkward taste'. The grounds, which are ten miles round, are the embodiment of power and wealth, underpinned by a reassuring sense of harmony and stability. Elizabeth's prize is much more than a romantic attachment. Georgiana is another pleasing reflection of Darcy's influence.

Miss Bingley shows her desperation by openly criticising Elizabeth in the crudest of terms. Previously, Darcy had dismissed Caroline's attacks with dead-pan **irony** (see Literary Terms). His uncharacteristic outburst is a measure of the passions that are boiling beneath the surface.

CHAPTERS 46–48

Elizabeth's world collapses when she receives two letters from Jane with the news that Lydia has eloped with

SCANDAL STRIKES THE BENNET HOUSEHOLD

Elizabeth's feels bitter that Lydia's flighty and headstrong character has been indulged by her parents.

Wickham and, as far as anyone can determine, they are not married. It is believed that they are living somewhere in London. Trembling from the shock, Elizabeth's first thought is to seek her uncle, but at that moment Darcy enters. Darcy is plainly alarmed and concerned for Elizabeth's welfare but he cannot offer any easy comfort. In her shame and despair, Elizabeth realises that she could love Darcy, but that chance is now lost forever.

The dinner at Pemberley is cancelled and Darcy leaves readily promising not to reveal anything of what has happened. Elizabeth and the Gardiners immediately depart for Longbourn.

Elizabeth is frank about her family.

On the journey back to Longbourn, Mr Gardiner tries to evaluate the seriousness of the situation. Elizabeth doubts whether Wickham has any intention of marrying Lydia. She candidly lays much of the blame on her father whom she thinks has made no attempt to correct Lydia's waywardness, although when the regiment were at Meryton there were no signs of any particular familiarity between Wickham and her sister.

The family are in a state of consternation and helplessness.

On their arrival, Jane is unable to add any further news. Mr Bennet is in London attempting to trace the couple but so far there has been no word. Mrs Bennet is hysterical and blames everyone but herself. When Mr Gardiner proposes returning to London to assist his brother-in-law, she can think of nothing but Lydia's wedding clothes and being bereaved and homeless when Wickham kills her husband. Mary has some bookish reflections, whilst Kitty is somewhat sobered by the fact that she, in fact, had known of Lydia's attachment for some time.

Lydia's shocking frivolity is highlighted.

Colonel Foster has visited, bearing a letter Lydia had sent his wife. In it Lydia treats the whole affair as a delightful joke and fully expects that she and Wickham will be married. Despite her criticisms, Elizabeth feels for her father and despairs of maintaining any vestiges of the family reputation.

Longbourn is plunged into a state of hopelessness. The expected letter from Mr Bennet is not forthcoming and a flood of local stories about Wickham's evil ways only serves to emphasise the misery. Mr Collins's letter of condolence simply expresses his condemnation of the family and his relief at not having married into it. Eventually, Mr Bennet gives up his search and returns home dispirited and acknowledging his own guilt in the affair. However, he still cannot resist teasing Kitty by declaring that he will be very severe on her in the future.

Mr Bennet is briefly remorseful but remains unchanged in his ways.

COMMENT   After the harmony of Pemberley with its reassuring sense of well-being, Lydia's elopement strikes a sharply discordant note. It also emphasises the gulf between the two moral orders of Pemberley and Longbourn, a divide which Elizabeth now despairs of ever crossing.

Mrs Bennet's indiscriminate talk of Mr Bennet's murder and Lydia's wedding dress in the same breath, is wildly comic but emphasises her moral bankruptcy.

CHAPTERS 49–50

The clouds begin to lift when a letter arrives from Mr Gardiner. He has found the couple, who are not yet married, but Wickham has agreed to a very modest settlement which requires Mr Bennet to lay out very little money indeed. Mr Bennet suspects that his brother-in-law has paid Wickham a very much larger sum to induce him to marry Lydia and does not know how he can pay him back.

Mrs Bennet is naturally overjoyed when she learns of her daughter's impending marriage and her thoughts immediately turn to clothes. She dismisses any generosity on her brother's part as no more than is due

THE TIDE BEGINS TO TURN

to them. Elizabeth is not hopeful of Lydia's chances of happiness but accepts that the situation could have been much worse.

Mrs Bennet's hysteria changes to joy.

Mr Bennet is troubled by the burden of indebtedness to his brother-in-law but is relieved that his immediate expenses will be slight. We learn that he has been financially imprudent in the past and made no provision for the eventuality of having no male heir. Mrs Bennet makes extravagant plans for the newly-weds to settle locally in a fine house, but she is outraged when Mr Bennet refuses even to spend any money on Lydia. To her, such neglect eclipses the shame of her daughter's behaviour. Elizabeth's thoughts turn to Darcy. She is regretful that she had told him of Lydia's actions, although she doubts whether Darcy would want to be associated with her family under any circumstances. She has come to understand what it is to be Darcy and appreciate his generous spirit. She longs that the clock could be turned back, for now he is lost to her, she knows that she loves him.

Mr Gardiner writes with the latest news that Wickham has accepted a permanent army post in the north and that his debts are in the process of being discharged.

Mr Bennet's weakness is shown once again.

Mr Bennet backs down on his decision never to allow Lydia and Wickham to enter Longbourn.

Elizabeth acknowledges, for the first time, that she loves Darcy.

COMMENT

In some respects Chapters 49–50 balance Chapters 46–8. The situation changes from one of utter despair to one that offers some hope, highlighting Mrs Bennet's violent change of mood but also in Elizabeth's relief that the situation could be much worse.

GLOSSARY

Chapter 50

the regulars regiments which had fixed barracks as opposed to the Militia which moved around

ensigncy the lowest grade of officer in the infantry

A

Identify the speaker and the person 'to whom' this comment refers.

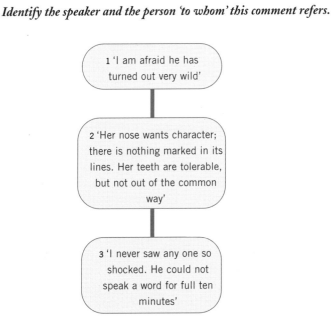

1 'I am afraid he has turned out very wild'

2 'Her nose wants character; there is nothing marked in its lines. Her teeth are tolerable, but not out of the common way'

3 'I never saw any one so shocked. He could not speak a word for full ten minutes'

Check your answers on page 96.

B

Consider these issues.

a How Jane Austen presents Lydia's character.

b How Elizabeth's perceptions of her family confirm Darcy's judgement.

c Elizabeth's feelings towards Wickham now that she knows the truth.

d Why Pemberley and its grounds make such an impression on Elizabeth.

e The ways in which an unsuspected side to Darcy's character is presented.

f Darcy's reaction to the news of Lydia's elopement.

g How the members of the Bennet family handle the news of the elopement.

h Why the news is especially painful for Elizabeth.

DARCY'S DRAMATIC INTERVENTION

CHAPTERS 51–52

Lydia is totally unrepentant and lacking in tact.

Elizabeth tries to put herself in Lydia's shoes and imagine the shame and embarrassment she would feel. Lydia's arrival at Longbourn after her wedding is attended by no such feelings, however. She is brash and brazen and, far from showing any remorse, boasts of her married state, even declaring that she now takes precedence over Jane at the dinner table.

Elizabeth's disgust at Lydia's vulgarity is soon displaced by her astonishment when her sister lets slip that Darcy was present at her wedding. Consumed with curiosity, she writes to Mrs Gardiner enquiring after the truth.

Darcy's discretion is demonstrated once again.

Significantly, Elizabeth not only feels indebted to Darcy but proud of him.

Her aunt writes back that it was, in fact, Darcy who tracked down the couple. He soon discovered that, whatever Lydia's hopes may have been, Wickham had no intention of marrying her. After much wrangling, Darcy succeeded in coming to a financial accommodation with Wickham, so that he would agree to marry Lydia. Darcy talked over the arrangements with Mr Gardiner but refused to allow him to make any contribution. However, in order to conceal his role in the affair, Darcy persuaded Mr Gardiner to take the credit for the settlement.

The pointed irony of Elizabeth's observations such as 'things are strangely misrepresented' cannot be lost on Wickham.

Elizabeth finds herself astonished on Darcy's behalf; she knows what it must have taken to have gone to such lengths to help a woman 'whom he must abominate and despise' and a man 'whom he always most wished to avoid'. For a fleeting moment, Elizabeth dares to think that he might have done all this for her. Her thoughts are interrupted by Wickham who once again attempts to find out how much she knows of his past. This time, Elizabeth is less guarded and her pointed replies leave Wickham in little doubt that his deceit has been exposed. Even so, seemingly unable to feel or express any remorse, Wickham kisses Elizabeth's hand as though they are the best of friends.

COMMENT From a narrative **point of view** (see Literary Terms) the elopement is a device to force Darcy and Elizabeth apart and then to throw them together again. In purely realistic terms, it would have been perfectly feasible for Darcy to have proposed at Pemberley but that would have led to rather a limp ending. The novel needs a dramatic **denouement** (see Literary Terms), a sense of danger and threat averted before the final celebrations.

Out of a sense of responsibility, if not respect, towards her youngest sister, Elizabeth treats Wickham with good humour. Her skilful management of their last conversation enables her to draw a veil over his past iniquities, while making it abundantly clear that she is fully acquainted with their nature.

CHAPTERS 53–55

No sooner than the newly-weds have departed for Newcastle, than it is strongly rumoured that Bingley will shortly be returning to Netherfield. At first Mrs Bennet expresses total indifference to Bingley but, before long, she is anxious to be the first to invite him to dinner. Jane plainly still feels for Bingley and is disturbed by the prospect of seeing him again, despite her assurances to the contrary. Having seen him at Pemberley, Elizabeth is reasonably convinced that Bingley is still drawn to her sister but she is uncertain that he is a free agent in the matter. Soon after his arrival, Bingley presents himself at Longbourn accompanied, to everyone's surprise, by Mr Darcy.

The return of Bingley, accompanied by Darcy, is a kind of rerun of the opening scenes of the novel.

Torn between hope and terror, Elizabeth buries herself in her needlework, hardly daring to look up. Jane is no less uneasy. Darcy seems less at ease than he had been in Derbyshire and barely speaks but he endures Mrs Bennet's intolerable rudeness with composure.

BINGLEY AND DARCY RETURN

*For once,
Elizabeth's
confidence deserts
her.*

*Not daring to
extend their hopes,
both sisters are
unwilling to
admit to their true
feelings.*

*Elizabeth now
appears to agree
with Charlotte's
earlier view that
'Jane should make
the most of every
half hour in which
she can command
his attention'
(p. 22).*

Elizabeth is once again covered in shame at her mother's behaviour but is heartened as Bingley becomes increasingly attentive to Jane.

After the gentlemen have left, Elizabeth is left pondering Darcy's motives in making the visit and decides to give him no further thought, whilst Jane declares that she can now treat Bingley merely as an acquaintance. The next time the two gentlemen visit, Bingley shows his continuing attachment to Jane but Elizabeth, who has been building her hopes on Darcy's showing some clear sign of his continuing interest in her, is disappointed. He seems strangely distant and they exchange scarcely more than a few passing words. Elizabeth becomes almost cross with Jane for refusing to recognise Bingley's affection.

Darcy leaves for London but is due to return in ten days. Meanwhile, Bingley becomes a regular visitor and Mrs Bennet is so encouraged by his attentiveness that she contrives to leave him alone with Jane. At first, her comic subterfuge is not rewarded: the hoped-for proposal is not forthcoming. Before long, however, Jane declares her happiness. Elizabeth wryly reflects on how all the attempts to frustrate this relationship have finally come to nought. She is delighted for Jane, confident in the belief that Bingley's affection is 'rationally founded' and that the couple are ideally matched.

Jane's joy is tempered slightly by her concern for Elizabeth's future happiness. Elizabeth, with characteristic resilience and good humour, reassures her sister that a second Mr Collins may yet appear.

Darcy's apparent avoidance of Elizabeth shows his underlying shyness and how nervous he is that he should be rejected once again.

Elizabeth dares not believe that Darcy can still love her.

GLOSSARY   *Chapter 53*

country a district, part of the country

CHAPTERS **56–57**

Events take a surprising turn with the sudden and unannounced arrival of Lady Catherine at the gates of Longbourn. She sweeps in and, after some disparaging remarks about the house and gardens, demands an interview with Elizabeth. As they make their way to a private corner of the garden, Elizabeth wonders how she could possibly have imagined that this arrogant, overbearing woman was at all like Darcy. It transpires that Lady Catherine has been informed that Darcy and Elizabeth intend to marry and she has come to demand that Elizabeth denies the report, although she is convinced it must be false. Elizabeth refuses to be browbeaten by Lady Catherine and responds to her attempts at intimidation with composure. The emptiness of Lady Catherine's accusations and threats are exposed and countered with characteristic alertness and skill.

Lady Catherine is no match for Elizabeth's skill in handling her coarse accusations and attempts at intimidation.

Despite their failings Elizabeth resents any attempt by Lady Catherine to disparage her family.

Elizabeth is clearly incensed by Lady Catherine's arrogance but maintains her dignity in the face of an onslaught on her character and breeding. Eventually, however, Elizabeth declares that she will be insulted no longer and brings the interview to a close. To Elizabeth's relief, her mother believes that the 'very fine-looking' woman was merely making a courtesy call.

Elizabeth is left to speculate on the extraordinary visit. Despite her strong-willed resistance to Lady Catherine's threats and demands, she is disturbed by the encounter. She guesses that the rumour of her engagement to Darcy had begun with the Lucases and reached Lady Catherine via Charlotte and Mr Collins. She is less certain about Darcy's response to pressure from his aunt. She fears that he may well be swayed by arguments concerning his loss of status and dignity.

Mr Bennet shows Elizabeth a letter he has just received from Mr Collins warning of the 'evils' which will follow from the anticipated betrothal of Darcy and Elizabeth. He is highly amused by the notion of Elizabeth being in any way attracted to a man who had probably never *Elizabeth feels* looked at her in his life and invites his daughter to *isolated.* share in his hilarity. Elizabeth responds politely, but when her father stumbles on the truth by asking whether Lady Catherine had called to withhold her consent, she feels hurt and isolated, since no-one can even suspect her true feelings.

C OMMENT Lady Catherine's dramatic intervention does, of course, **ironically** (see Literary Terms) precipitate the very marriage she is attempting to avert. The confrontation can also be viewed as a clash of the old order and the new. Lady Catherine, steeped in her aristocratic past, can only threaten and talk angrily about honour, decorum and prudence. Elizabeth, however, is coolly rational, skilfully demolishing each of Lady Catherine's charges in turn. Elizabeth takes command by virtue of her integrity and the scope of her intelligence.

CHAPTERS 58–61

Elizabeth, considering Lady Catherine's influence with her nephew, rather expects Darcy to send his apologies and fail to return as promised but her hopes revive when, before long, Bingley brings him to Longbourn. The party set off on a walk and Elizabeth finds herself alone in Darcy's company. Unable to stand the tension any longer, she takes the initiative and broaches the subject of his intervention in the affair of Wickham and Lydia. As though relieved of a burden by being able to share the truth, he explains that his actions were entirely for her sake and that his love is undimmed. They walk on, gradually unfolding the development of their feelings towards one another. Ironically, what finally brought them together was Lady Catherine's attempt to force them apart. When she told Darcy of Elizabeth's stubborn refusal to give in to her demands, he dared hope once again that his feelings were not in vain.

The ice is finally broken.

Together, they explore the twists and turns of their relationship. Darcy admits that he had been stung by Elizabeth's justified accusation that he had behaved in an ungentlemanly manner. For her part, she confesses her wilful and headstrong character had blinded her to the truth. It emerges that Darcy has not only endorsed Bingley's attachment to Jane but apologises for and agrees that his previous interference was 'impertinent'.

Elizabeth may remember Darcy's claim that he takes pains to avoid any possibility of being ridiculed.

By the end of the walk, the couple's previous differences have melted away but Elizabeth restrains herself from making a joke at Darcy's expense, remembering that he has yet to learn how to be teased.

The skies may have cleared for Elizabeth but she is still left with the question of how to inform her unsuspecting family. Even Jane, who is the first to be informed, reacts in astonishment and disbelief, so convinced was she of Elizabeth's thorough dislike of Darcy. Elizabeth explains that she could not discuss her confused feelings for Darcy without having to mention Bingley. Jane clears Elizabeth of the charge of slyness and the two sisters talk well into the night.

ALL'S WELL THAT ENDS WELL

The next morning, to Mrs Bennet's expressed disgust, Darcy reappears. The couple agree that the parents' permission to marry should be sought without delay. On hearing the news, Mr Bennet is shocked and anxious that his daughter has not made a dreadful mistake. Elizabeth reassures her father who frankly admits that, in any case, he has already given his consent because he is too overawed by Mr Darcy to refuse him anything. When Elizabeth speaks to her mother she is, for once, speechless but the thought of ten thousand pounds a year soon dispels her professed dislike of Darcy.

The lovers review their emotions.

Now that everything is settled, Elizabeth begins to enjoy her new situation and quizzes Darcy on the progress of his love for her. She learns that he admired her for the liveliness of her mind and that the reason for his reticence on his recent visits to Longbourn was simply embarrassment. She admits to the same sensation and they rejoice in recalling how the ice was finally broken.

There follows an exchange of letters:

- Elizabeth writes to Mrs Gardiner expressing her unconfined joy
- Mr Bennet writes a short letter to Mr Collins confirming the engagement, advising him that his interests lie with Mr Darcy rather than Lady Catherine
- Miss Bingley sends her congratulations but her insincerity is clear even to Jane. By contrast, Miss Darcy writes warmly, expressing genuine delight

Before long Mr Collins and Charlotte come to stay at Lucas Lodge, the latter relieved to escape Lady Catherine's ill-temper. Darcy manages to withstand Mr Collins's obsequiousness and Sir William's extravagant compliments but Elizabeth finds it necessary to protect him from Mrs Philips's vulgarity. The removal to

Pemberley is looked forward to as a relief from such unwelcome attentions.

The marriage of Elizabeth has wide and mainly beneficial effects.

The lives of all members of the families concerned are altered in some way by the marriages. The possible exception is Mrs Bennet who, despite having her wildest dreams fulfilled, remains as silly as ever, so much so, that Bingley and Jane feel obliged to escape her attentions by moving to Derbyshire, happily within easy reach of Pemberley. Mr Bennet misses Elizabeth deeply but compensates with frequent visits to Pemberley. In their different ways, recent events have a beneficial effect on the remaining daughters. Free of Lydia's influence, Kitty becomes much more sensible, whilst Mary breaks out of her shell and becomes more sociable. Lydia is still incorrigible and writes to Elizabeth demanding that Darcy should provide them with additional income. She and Wickham are constantly in debt and their relationship is distinctly cooling.

Miss Bingley prefers to make her peace with Elizabeth than to be excluded from Pemberley. Georgiana and Elizabeth become very close, though Georgiana never fails to wonder at Elizabeth's playful manner with her brother. Even Lady Catherine's anger is eventually supplanted by curiosity and she deigns to descend on Pemberley. Finally, Elizabeth's and Darcy's indebtedness to the Gardiners is reflected in their enduring closeness and affection.

COMMENT

The return of Darcy, encouraged by what he has heard from his aunt about Elizabeth's defiance, signals the final passage of the novel towards its resolution but not without some minor ripples of comic suspense. Elizabeth is exasperated at Jane's indifference to Bingley's obvious admiration and despite repeated visits and Mrs Bennet's contrivance, it seems that he will never propose. For her part, hope and fear transform her into a coy, blushing young woman, while Darcy becomes an awkward tongue-tied suitor.

Elizabeth and Darcy look back over the progress of their love.

Elizabeth's and Darcy's account of their love's progress offers a useful gloss on the novel's events.

The final chapter is a kind of mirror of a society which has achieved a state of relative equilibrium and stability. In effect, a quiet revolution has taken place: old prejudices have been banished by the formation of new alliances. The world may be an imperfect place and some things are not susceptible to improvement. Neither Mrs Bennet nor Lady Catherine will achieve true gentility and Lydia and Wickham will continue to pursue their flimsy dreams but Pemberley appears to offer a glimpse of an ideal world.

A constant thread that ran through the work of the eighteenth-century writers Jane Austen so admired was the pursuit of happiness and it may not be too fanciful to suggest that *Pride and Prejudice* celebrates that ideal. She was no revolutionary, but it is curious to note that the famous opening sentence offers a faint, if **ironic** (see Literary Terms), echo of the Declaration of American Independence: 'We hold these truths to be self-evident, that all men … are endowed by their Creator with certain unalienable Rights, that among these are Life, Liberty and the pursuit of Happiness.'

GLOSSARY   *Chapter 59*

pin money 'pocket money' that was given to wives for their personal expenses

special licence a licence that allowed the gentry to have a private wedding

TEST YOURSELF (Chapters 51–61)

A

Identify the speaker and the person 'to whom' this comment refers.

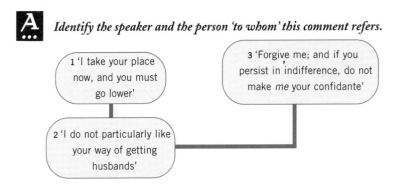

1 'I take your place now, and you must go lower'

2 'I do not particularly like your way of getting husbands'

3 'Forgive me; and if you persist in indifference, do not make *me* your confidante'

Identify the person 'to whom' this comment refers.

4 'was more than usually insolent and disagreeable'

5 'Never had his wit been directed in a manner so little agreeable to Elizabeth'

6 'had yet to learn to be laught at'

Check your answers on page 96.

B *Consider these issues.*

a What makes Lydia's behaviour on her return so shocking.

b The significance of Darcy's intervention in the affair of Wickham and Lydia.

c How Elizabeth treats Wickham.

d How Jane and Elizabeth feel and act on the reappearance of Bingley and Darcy.

e The skill with which Elizabeth deals with Lady Catherine.

f How the last conversations between Elizabeth and Darcy reflect on what has gone before.

PART THREE

COMMENTARY

THEMES

To reduce a novel by Jane Austen to a set of themes is necessarily to oversimplify and to abuse that 'delicacy' which her early admirer, Sir Walter Scott, so appreciated. Nevertheless, there are concerns or areas of interest that permeate her work. They are, however, subtly intertwined so that it is difficult to approach the novel from one **point of view** (see Literary Terms) without impinging on another viewpoint. The central focus is, of course, Elizabeth, and her 'character' is inseparable from the consideration of almost any aspect of the work.

LOVE AND MARRIAGE

We need to recognise the importance of 'romantic' love in all our lives.

At face value, *Pride and Prejudice* is a **romantic** (see Literary Terms) comedy and Jane Austen acknowledges how romantic feelings may overwhelm us. For couples in love, their joy can never be understated; their world is complete or, as one poet (John Donne) put it, 'nothing else is'. Few are immune. Lydia will never be happy without her 'angel' (p. 236), Wickham. Jane feels she is 'the happiest creature in the world' (p. 279), whilst Elizabeth declares she is 'happier even than Jane' (p. 300).

But whilst romantic passion needs to be celebrated, it offers an incomplete picture of human relationships. Jane Austen makes it clear that the passion of the moment is a poor foundation for lasting happiness. Mr Bennet had been 'captivated by youth and beauty' (p. 194) but Mrs Bennet's 'weak understanding and illiberal mind' (p. 194) prevented any lasting affection. By the end of the novel Lydia's and Wickham's reckless relationship has already descended into an existence which is 'unsettled in the extreme' (p. 311). Their marriage will not even be supported by the relative financial and social status that Mr and Mrs Bennet are able to enjoy.

Extreme views of love and marriage are unsatisfactory.

Charlotte by contrast is wholly unsentimental: 'I am not a romantic ... I ask only a comfortable home' (p. 105). Her readiness to settle for financial security to the exclusion of all other considerations, which so disturbs Elizabeth, is also not a basis for a true marriage. **Ironically** (see Literary Terms), like Mr Bennet, who retreats to his study, Charlotte soon learns to cope by using a back room so as to keep out of her husband's way.

If such marriages signify discord, the ideal relationship should signify harmony. Elizabeth approves of Jane and Bingley for just this reason; their happiness is not simply based on physical attraction but is 'rationally founded' and the couple possess a 'general similarity of feeling and taste' (p. 280). Likewise, Mr Gardiner's 'sensible, gentlemanlike' character is complemented by his wife's 'amiable, intelligent' (p. 118) personality.

The marriage of Elizabeth and Darcy, however, represents a much more complex state of affairs. Jane and Bingley's marriage is prudent on the basis of shared temperament and taste. Despite setbacks their feelings for each other do not change. By contrast, Elizabeth and Darcy achieve mutual admiration and

The basis of a true marriage.

respect only through the painful process of stripping away misunderstanding and self-deception, as they reveal to each other in Chapter 58. Their marriage is rational because they have learned to know *why* they love each other and it is secure because it is hard-won (see also Context & Setting and Characters).

THE ROLE OF WOMEN

Note Jane Austen's resistance to women playing a wholly subservient role.

In the conventional society of Jane Austen's day, a woman's role was fairly clear. Put most crudely, her position in life was defined by her father or her husband and she was expected to be modest, submissive and incapable of independent thought. With few exceptions, their education was inferior to their male contemporaries. Jane Austen was, of course, part of that society and in many respects the very form and subject of her novels would seem to accept women's traditional role. She is not, however, uncritical. Ignorance is certainly not bliss in Jane Austen's world; moral deficiency is closely linked with a narrowness of outlook, often compounded by lack of intelligence. It is easy to laugh at Mrs Bennet's 'fidgets' and her wild changes of mood but she remains a 'woman of mean understanding' (p. 7) who is incapable of exercising any moral discrimination. Lydia's 'animal spirits' (p. 40) are likewise linked to the fact that she is 'vain, ignorant, idle' (p. 190). The simpering Caroline Bingley and the overbearing Lady Catherine also reveal their cultural poverty when they display their lack of genuine interest in reading and music. The comfortable Charlotte does not lack intelligence but she sacrifices her individuality by marrying Mr Collins.

Much of this ignorance we see through Elizabeth's eyes. She cannot abide small talk ('Their table was superlatively stupid. Scarcely a syllable was uttered that did not relate to the game'), preferring the greater stimulus of conversational fencing with the gentlemen.

Consider the importance of independent thought to Elizabeth and Darcy.

The characterisation of Elizabeth seems to represent something of a departure from the conventional image of women at that time. Above all, she possesses **wit** (see Literary Terms), intelligence and an independence of thought that sets her apart, even from her elder sister. It has been argued that the picture we have of

Elizabeth reflects the views of thinkers such as Mary Wollstonecraft, whose pioneering writing on women's rights argued that in order to aspire to equality, women should devote their energies to reason and independent thought.

However, it would be wrong to suggest that Elizabeth entirely represents 'new woman'. Despite her misgivings, she is a dutiful daughter and whilst she was prepared to reject one of the richest men in England, ultimately she is anxious to assume her role as mistress of Pemberley: 'she looked forward with delight to the time when they should be removed from society so little pleasing to either, to all the comfort and elegance of their family party at Pemberley' (p. 309).

The desirability of belonging to the 'gentry' cannot be overlooked.

SOCIAL AND MORAL PERSPECTIVE

The distinction between gentry and trade is closely interwoven into the novel's social relationships. Darcy prides himself on being a gentleman with all the duties and obligations that his status entails. And, as Caroline Bingley constantly reminds him, he would be lowering himself by associating with the Bennet family as they are connected with trade. Elizabeth, however, strongly asserts her dignity when she tells Lady Catherine 'He (Darcy) is a gentleman; I am a gentleman's daughter; so far we are equal' (p. 287). Conversely, the high-minded Miss Bingley forgets that the source of the family fortune, on which their status is founded, is trade. Sir William Lucas's background is also in trade but he devotes all his energies in proving his credentials to be a country gentleman. By contrast, Mr and Mrs Gardiner make no apologies for their participation in trade yet display a true gentility that impresses Mr Darcy.

Lady Catherine, however, displays a vulgarity wholly unworthy of her social position. Throughout *Pride and Prejudice*, Jane Austen sets moral status against social

Consider the importance of social and moral status.

status. Much of Elizabeth's initial antipathy to Darcy can be seen as revulsion that, in his supposed treatment of Wickham, his moral standards are not worthy of his standing in society. The corollary is that Darcy, whilst 'bewitched' by Elizabeth, cannot rid himself of thoughts of her social inferiority.

Charlotte seeks a comfortable compromise but although she acquires the social advantage of being a clergyman's wife she 'sacrificed every better feeling' (p. 105). While Georgiana possesses the social advantage, her shy, unassuming demeanour belies her status and wealth. Mr Collins may seem to be no more than a figure of fun but his absurdity may also expose the dangers of social respectability without social and moral responsibility. In gaining a position in the Church, he has succeeded where Wickham failed, but for all the outward differences in their personalities, they both put self-interest before concern for others.

Note how the novel sugggests how society may change for the better.

It is interesting to observe that the plot's resolution is brought about by moral alliances that cross class boundaries. The gentleman, Darcy, conspires with the tradesman, Mr Gardiner, to rescue Lydia and the Bennets from social disgrace. Some may object that Elizabeth enjoys the best of two worlds; she has the pleasure of rejecting Darcy and the pleasure of accepting him. Her conversion to the material joys of Pemberley seems inconsistent with her criticisms of Charlotte's preoccupation with financial security. Such a change of heart is demanded by the conventions of the **romantic** novel (see Literary Terms), but in Jane Austen's scheme of things, the marriage of Elizabeth and Darcy may also represent an enrichment and rejuvenation of the traditional social order. Elizabeth's assertiveness is redirected so as to invest Pemberley, and all that it stands for, with a new sense of purpose (see also Context & Setting).

PRIDE AND PREJUDICE

It is not difficult to find *examples* of these characteristics. Darcy is excessively proud of his social standing and his sense of superiority engenders a prejudiced view of Elizabeth and her kind. Conversely Elizabeth and the neighbourhood take against Darcy from the outset. Whether this prejudice stems from hurt pride or small-town suspicion of those with power and influence, it seriously colours Elizabeth's judgement.

Exaggerated pride is perhaps displayed most clearly by Lady Catherine and blind prejudice by Mrs Bennet but we should guard against treating pride and prejudice as simple labels that we attach to characters and their behaviour. Jane Austen takes a far more complex view of human nature.

'Pride' has many aspects in the novel.

First, neither pride nor prejudice are fixed attributes of human beings, nor are they always distinguishable from other human characteristics. Tucked away in one of the novel's less significant corners, is an observation by the bookish Mary on the subject of pride: 'Vanity and pride are different things ... A person may be proud without being vain. Pride relates more to our opinion of ourselves, vanity to what others think of us' (p. 20). As ever, Mary is ignored, but her declaration deserves examination. We may see that when Lady Catherine appeals to Elizabeth's sense of 'honour', 'decorum' and 'prudence' (p. 286), she is not so much taking pride in her high moral standards as displaying her vanity by trying to protect her basest interests in a most aggressive and arrogant way. Similarly, Caroline Bingley's 'superciliousness' and snobbery towards almost everybody, thinly disguised by her outward charm, soon merges into jealousy towards Elizabeth. Her transparent attempts to ingratiate herself with Darcy reveal the true vulgarity that hides behind the proud public face.

Mr Collins's inflated pride in his own true worth is easily seen as no more than vanity and conceit and even the amiable Sir William Lucas's understandable pride in his title is a gentle vanity. Lady Catherine, Caroline, Mr Collins and Sir William all exhibit the kind of pride that Mary identifies as vanity; essentially, they are most concerned with their public image.

Charlotte is rather different: she displays no vanity but in agreeing to marry Mr Collins, Elizabeth feels she has disgraced herself. Charlotte lacks personal pride and shows a readiness to compromise her judgement in a way that Elizabeth would never entertain.

How we judge others is an important theme of the book.

There is another side to the question, however, which is concerned with how we judge others. *Pride and Prejudice* is based on an earlier novel, which has not survived, called *First Impressions*. The title is helpful because it alerts us to the dangers of making crude judgements about people without knowing enough about them. To do so is to invite prejudice. Elizabeth rushes to damn Darcy on insufficient evidence and she is also ready to judge him in the simplest possible terms. Darcy *is* proud but Elizabeth mistakes his proud manner for the kind of patronising arrogance displayed by his aunt. The way they treat their tenants makes the difference clear: Darcy cares, Lady Catherine interferes.

Jane Austen goes even further to suggest that how well we know others is also dependent on how well we know ourselves. Elizabeth is predisposed to be won over by the rakish Wickham, because of her prejudices towards Darcy. When the truth emerges, she has to admit to herself how her powers of judgement had failed her (see Chapter 36).

Darcy, too, reassesses his pride in both mind and deed. He sets his dignity aside to come to the aid of Lydia and Wickham and lays bare his mistaken understanding of himself to Elizabeth: 'I was given good principles, but left to follow them in pride and conceit' (p. 297).

The conclusion we must draw is that rational love is selfless and devoid of any vain pride and thoughtless prejudice, but to achieve that state one must first know oneself.

STRUCTURE

Look at how Jane Austen uses a typical romantic plot.

Jane Austen based her plot on the familiar format of the **romantic** novel (see Literary Terms): the heroine, who is lively and attractive but not glamorous, becomes acquainted with the hero who is in some way mysterious or even threatening. She is repulsed but he is captivated. Events and feelings force them apart but the reader knows they are really being drawn together. For a while, she is distracted by a false lover but when his wickedness is exposed, her eyes are opened to the hero's virtues. But it all seems too late; there are insuperable obstacles to their ever being united, until that is, the hero secretly takes decisive action and intervenes.

Key episodes

There are a number of key episodes and events – the two balls, the extended visit to Netherfield, Wickham's revelations, Bingley's sudden return to London – leading up to Darcy's proposal that turns Elizabeth against him. His letter and the visit to Pemberley transform her feelings but Lydia's sudden elopement appears to snatch happiness from her grasp. Darcy's decisive intervention and Elizabeth's equally decisive defiance of Lady Catherine rescue her from the brink.

The structure, however, is not simply to do with Elizabeth and Darcy. The plot and the themes overlap and intertwine in a fascinating variety of ways. The main romance runs in parallel with the romance of Bingley and Jane. The marriage of Charlotte and Mr

Collins both deepens our understanding of the theme of marriage and provides the vital narrative link with Lady Catherine.

Also important to the design of the novel are the two major changes of scene: the visits to Kent and Derbyshire. As well as creating interest for the reader through the introduction of new situations and characters, they offer new moral and emotional perspectives.

CHARACTERS

ELIZABETH BENNET

Vivacious

Engaging

Strong-willed

Thoughtful

Witty

Caring

Perceptive

Elizabeth Bennet stands at the centre of the novel. She is the heroine but also the eyes through which we see and judge most of what happens. She is less beautiful than her elder sister, Jane, but has a natural vivacity and an endearing lack of stuffiness. She lacks Jane's reserve and **ironically** (see Literary Terms) shares something of Lydia's wilfulness, if not her waywardness. She is the favourite of Mr Bennet and she inherits his sense of the ridiculous. For instance, Mr Collins's introductory letter leaves them both in amused amazement: 'Can he be a sensible man, sir?' (p. 56).

Mr Bennet recognises her 'quickness' and Mr Darcy admires the 'liveliness' of her mind. Certainly she relishes the cut and thrust of stimulating conversation and is always prepared to cross swords with the mighty Darcy. In Chapter 11, for instance, responding to one of Darcy's provocative remarks, Caroline titters 'How shall we punish him for such a speech?' (p. 50). It is Elizabeth, however, who rises to the challenge. The reader, of course, knows that it is at such moments that Elizabeth is unconsciously drawn to Darcy. However much she may resent him, his proud, Olympian manner speaks of wider horizons and richer stimulus than Longbourn can offer. It is noticeable that she takes little part in the everyday chit-chat of her mother and her younger sisters and she shows no interest in their regular visits to the local milliner's.

Look at the many sides of Elizabeth's character.

She is also a strong-minded person who will not compromise her principles and self-belief. She is reluctant to place marriage at the centre of her ambitions without any regard for feelings and circumstances. She is shocked by Charlotte's single-minded vision of marriage and she has no hesitation in rejecting two financially advantageous proposals.

Her strength of character is matched by her insight and sensitivity. For example, she is quick to penetrate the Bingley sisters' superficial civility and shares the pain that Jane must feel when she eventually accepts the truth about her false friend. In fact, her own feelings and attitudes are tightly bound up with concern for her elder sister. The first reason she offers for rejecting Darcy is that he had ruined 'perhaps for ever, the happiness of a most beloved sister' (p. 158). Later, even though she is on tenterhooks concerning Darcy's feelings towards her, she is still deeply anxious for Jane's happiness and is delighted when she sees that Bingley must still love her.

For all her readiness to argue her corner and act in ways that Caroline Bingley, for instance, considers unladylike, her behaviour is always civilised, with a lack of affectation and pretence that is the sign of true good-breeding. As a consequence, her awareness of her family's deficiencies is acute. Her mother's and Lydia's ignorant vulgarity is a source of continuing shame but her sensitivity to Mr Bennet's weakness and lack of parental control is even more painful. Darcy's reflections on her family's 'total want of propriety' (p. 163) only serve to confirm her perceptions.

At the same time, she is nothing less than a loyal and respectful daughter. She has the family's interests at

heart when she tries to dissuade her father from
allowing Lydia to go to Brighton but she accepts his
misguided decision without further question. The affair
of Lydia is especially wounding to Elizabeth: 'the
mischief of neglect and mistaken indulgence towards
such a girl. – Oh! how acutely did she feel it!' (p. 227).
Her shame is intensified by thoughts of what Darcy
must think, and despair of him ever again having any
regard for her. Even so, she is still able to feel sorry for
her father and when Lady Catherine confronts her with
the scandal, she is fiercely loyal. She takes the attack on
her youngest sister as a personal insult and firmly
dismisses her Ladyship.

Don't forget
Elizabeth does
have faults.

For all her maturity and clear-sightedness Elizabeth
does, of course, completely misjudge Darcy. The
transformation of her 'prejudice' against him into 'pride'
in his character and achievements, is the subject of the
novel's central narrative thread. The painful process
from dislike to admiration and love, reveals Elizabeth's
ability to overcome her indignation and subject herself
to ruthless self-examination. She does not simply *react*
to Darcy's letter, she *analyses* it. All of which leaves
open the question of how she could delude herself so
comprehensively in the first instance. The simple
answer is hurt pride stemming from Darcy's disparaging
remarks at the first assembly. However, to nurture a
grudge or to dwell on a passing remark is not in
Elizabeth's character; she is even able to behave with
tolerable good-humour towards Wickham after his
unforgiveable behaviour.

A more interesting answer is that Darcy's apparent
disdain represents a challenge to her individuality.
Wickham's easy charms and cheap flattery, offer a brief
diversion but, from the outset, it is Darcy who engages
her energies most profoundly. His proud manner sparks
her defiance, which in turn engages his admiration. At

the conclusion of the tale, Elizabeth herself analyses her attractions for Darcy: 'The fact is, that you were sick of civility, of deference, of officious attention. You were disgusted with women who were always speaking and looking, and thinking for *your* approbation alone. I roused, and interested you, because I was so unlike *them*' (p. 306).

Ultimately, it is her resilience and sense of humour that distinguishes Elizabeth and enables her to see her affairs in a sane and civilised perspective – 'I dearly love a laugh' (p. 50). The one wifely task that she sets herself is to nurture Darcy's underdeveloped sense of humour.

MR DARCY

Aloof
Reserved
Assured
Shy
Decisive
Responsible

Mr Darcy is immensely rich and powerful. He is a man of the world, who thinks nothing of travelling fifty miles in half a day, an unimaginable feat for most people of the time. In modern terms, he would be a leading member of the jet-set. Such people can easily arouse resentment and he is no exception: the people of Meryton soon mark him down as 'haughty', 'reserved' and 'the proudest, most disagreeable man in the world' (p. 12). He is, however, well qualified as a romantic hero. There is an air of assurance about him and even a sense of danger in his cold manner. However, he attributes his reserve to his natural shyness, whilst his housekeeper maintains it is because he does not wish to show off like other young men. Nevertheless, he does not suffer fools gladly and by his own admission his 'good opinion, once lost is lost for ever' (p. 51). There is, of course, much at Longbourn and Meryton to provoke his intolerance. Apart from the general narrowness of country life (Chapter 9), he has Mrs Bennet's embarrassing coarseness, Sir William's overfamiliarity, Mr Collins's lack of decorum and, although not directed at him, Lydia's impertinent reminder of Bingley's promise to mount a ball. More seriously, his concerns about the Bennet family's social inferiority cause him to 'detach' Bingley from Jane and outrage Elizabeth when first he proposes to her. He treats Mrs Bennet's rudeness with silent disdain and Mr Collins's uninvited attentions with 'distant civility' (p. 83), but he also has a dry and economical wit (see Literary Terms) that can readily dispose of those who should know better. For instance, Caroline Bingley's brainless attempts at flattery (Chapter 10) are dismissed with dead-pan politeness.

Compare the public and private faces of Mr Darcy. As with all romantic heroes, there is a hidden side to Darcy, which is revealed when Elizabeth visits Pemberley. The other, positive aspect of his pride is a sense of duty to ensure the well-being of those in his charge. He is well-loved by his employees and tenants; the warmth of his love for his sister is plain to see and to Elizabeth's 'astonishment' (p. 203) she learns that his housekeeper never had a cross word from him in her life.

However, his pride in his status and his pride in his sense of responsibility become confused in his treatment of Bingley. Eventually, he has to admit that his attempts to interfere in Bingley's life had been 'impertinent' (p. 298). The key to the realisation that he had been 'selfish and overbearing' (p. 297) is Elizabeth's accusation that he had not behaved in a gentleman-like manner. Through Elizabeth's prompting, he learns that while status is important, in the last analysis, true breeding is not dependent on rank.

JANE BENNET Miss Bennet is the eldest of the sisters and the most handsome. She has a serene personality that always seeks to see the best in everybody. This generous outlook, in many ways so admirable, proves the source of her own distress. Her misplaced trust in Caroline

Handsome
Gentle
Generous
Vulnerable

Bingley leaves Jane exposed and unsuspecting of the true reasons for Bingley's absence. However, Jane proves wiser than Elizabeth when she feels certain that there must be more to the relationship between Wickham and Darcy than first appears.

Jane and Elizabeth have a close relationship

Throughout the novel Jane and Elizabeth maintain a close and loving relationship. In fact, it sometimes seems as if Elizabeth is the elder sister, such is Jane's apparent innocence in the ways of the world. It is Charlotte that points out that Jane is too diffident and inclined to hide her feelings (Chapter 6). Elizabeth defends her sister at the time but later has to agree with Darcy about her sister's apparent 'indifference' to Bingley. Jane is stoical about her disappointment in love but Elizabeth is able to see her true misery. Such is her lack of confidence, that to the near despair of Elizabeth, she refuses to recognise that Bingley's renewed attentions on his return are anything more than signs of casual friendship. The interrupted but gentle romance of Jane and Bingley, in which simple, unassuming virtue is rewarded, forms a charming contrast to the more tempestuous affair of Elizabeth and Darcy.

MR BINGLEY Charles Bingley is the 'single man in possession of a good fortune' alluded to in the first sentence. In fact, it is not his wealth but his affable, unaffected and unassuming character that impresses. Unlike his friend Darcy and his sister Caroline, he is devoid of snobbery. He is not a reflective person, preferring to act on the spur of the moment, but he is loyal. Before meeting him, Mrs Gardiner is somewhat sceptical about the reported violence of his passions, but, in fact, his devotion to Jane is unwavering. However, he is too easily influenced. Darcy's snobbery and his sisters' maliciousness force Bingley and Jane apart. **Ironically** (see Literary Terms), it is Darcy's 'conversion' that opens the way for their reunion.

GEORGE WICKHAM

Wickham is a version of the corrupt, pleasure-loving rake who is an essential ingredient of the eighteenth-century **romantic** novel (see Literary Terms), somewhat watered down to suit the lighter, comic tone of *Pride and Prejudice*.

Smooth-talking
Entertaining
Deceitful
Mercenary
Unprincipled

Outwardly charming and plausible, he is an excellent conversationalist who engages everyone's sympathy for his supposed injustice at the hands of Darcy. The truth is that he is a cowardly spendthrift and a liar who is prepared to exploit women for personal pleasure and material gain. There is a hint of something particularly unsavoury about his attempted seduction of Georgiana and his elopement with Lydia, both of whom are attractive girls in their mid-teens. In both cases, it is Darcy who saves the young women from ruin.

MRS BENNET

Mrs Bennet is possibly Jane Austen's best-known comic character. Her obsession with marrying off her five daughters results in all kinds of absurdities, comic subterfuges, knowing winks and violent oscillations between depression and ecstasy. She is the centre of numerous scenes of acute embarrassment, such as the occasion she loudly professes her dislike of Mr Darcy within his earshot (Chapter 18).

Ignorant
Fickle
Talkative
Obsessed

Within the context of an essentially light-hearted story, Mrs Bennet, like Mr Collins, may seem mere **caricature** (see Literary Terms), but we need shift our **point of view** (see Literary Terms) only slightly to see her as a pernicious influence. Her ignorant and superficial outlook leaves her devoid of any moral discrimination. Her hysteria at Lydia's elopement is outwardly comic but her concern for her daughter's wedding clothes in such dire circumstances is chilling.

MR BENNET

Mr Bennet's easy wit (see Literary Terms) and his wry sense of life's absurdities, not least his wife, are initially attractive; his remarks are always entertaining. However, it is especially painful to his favourite daughter, Elizabeth, that he has neglected his duties as a father. He is always ready to humour, mock or tease but never to intervene. Elizabeth largely blames him for Lydia's precocious and uncontrolled behaviour.

His attempts to track down Wickham and Lydia are hopelessly ineffective; he even neglects to write. On his return from London, he blames himself at first but his mock sternness towards Kitty is an early indication he cannot take his responsibilities seriously.

For a man of such sharp wit, he is curiously insensitive. His quip about Jane being able to enjoy the privilege of having being jilted is amusing but also rather cruel. He also displays a certain lack of principle. He is worried about how he is to repay his brother-in-law for supposedly securing a settlement with Wickham but such scruples vanish immediately he learns of Darcy's part in the affair. Furthermore, we learn at the last that he is quite content to trespass on Darcy's and Elizabeth's generosity by arriving at Pemberley unannounced.

MR COLLINS

Pompous
Absurd
Concerted
Fawning
Self-opinionated
Mercenary

Mr Collins is well summed up by Elizabeth: 'Mr Collins is a conceited, pompous, narrow-minded, silly man'. From his smug, self-regarding and impertinent introductory letter, his presence in the novel is virtually an endless illustration of Elizabeth's judgement. His servile praise of Lady Catherine seems inexhaustible, although he appears to make very little distinction between his patron and her possessions; he even knows how many windows grace the façade of Rosings.

His self-importance is comic because it reveals itself in extraordinary long-winded speeches and ponderous attempts at social grace. He is, however, a rather nasty character, who only escapes the charge of hypocrisy because of his complete lack of self-awareness. His superficiality is seen in the ease with which he is able to propose to both Elizabeth and Charlotte in the space of less than a week! For a clergyman, he possesses not a vestige of spirituality. Mr Bennet relishes his absurdity but Mr Collins's advice that the Bennet family should disown Lydia exposes his capacity for malice. As in the case of so many of Jane Austen's **caricatures** (see Literary Terms), the comic ridicule entertains but also cuts into the darker side of human nature.

LADY CATHERINE DE BOURGH

Lady Catherine's overbearing arrogance and sense of her own dignity is evident in all she says and does. Her sense of her unquestionable authority and right to control people's lives is most sharply seen when she confronts Elizabeth about her rumoured engagement to Darcy. Her enjoyment of flattery is no less sickening than Mr Collins's enthusiasm to give it; Elizabeth's preparedness to disagree with her is received with incomprehension.

Her tastes are vulgar and ostentatious and her professed love of music is a sham. In many ways she is a kind of aristocratic Mrs Bennet, sharing with Elizabeth's mother a brashness and rudeness that stems from a lack of innate intelligence and breeding. Her attitudes and behaviour offer an illuminating contrast to Darcy's.

LYDIA BENNET

Lydia is the youngest of the five daughters and is fifteen when the novel opens. She is described as 'well-grown' with 'high animal spirits' (p. 40). Her smiling

face and confidently provocative manner make her very
attractive to men. She is totally selfish and her only
thought is for her own pleasure: 'In Lydia's
imagination, a visit to Brighton comprised every
possibility of happiness' (p. 190).

She is unaware how vulnerable she really is and she is
easy prey for one such as Wickham. However, she is
not the least chastened by her adventure and treats it all
as a huge joke. Least of all is she able to appreciate the
distress she has caused her family. She does, of course,
have the uncritical support of Mrs Bennet, whom she
so closely resembles.

CAROLINE BINGLEY

Miss Bingley's superficial civility thinly disguises her
bitchiness. She is rich, regards herself a member of the
social elite but lacks appropriate dignity and style. She
treats Jane abominably and jealously tries to discredit
Elizabeth in Darcy's eyes. However, her cheap jibes and
crude sarcasm serve only to emphasise her desperation
and have a counter-productive effect on Darcy.

CHARLOTTE LUCAS

*Charlotte
represents a
narrow but
important attitude
to marriage.*

Within the scheme of the novel, Charlotte is regarded
as a kind of failure and disappointment. In settling for
Mr Collins she appears to have compromised all
sensible principles in the quest for security and comfort.

Elizabeth is shocked but Charlotte possesses neither
Jane's beauty nor Elizabeth's confidence and **wit**
(see Literary Terms). Her pragmatic approach to
marriage may be restricted, but within the wider
context of society at large, it probably represents a more
realistic goal than that achieved by Elizabeth or Jane.
Charlotte is a sensible woman who seems well able to

adapt to her new circumstances. However much
Elizabeth may take pity on her, Charlotte's chosen lot
must be weighed against the fickle and itinerant
lifestyle of Lydia and Wickham.

LANGUAGE & STYLE

Jane Austen herself thought that *Pride and Prejudice* was
'rather too light and bright and sparkling'. Whether she
was right or not, the brilliance of her wit, her mastery
of nuance and tone and the effortless fluency of her
prose never fail to astound her readers.

Voices

Jane Austen's characters are perfectly imagined in the
way that they speak. For instance, Mr Bennet's dry wit
is outwardly genial but has a bitter edge to it that
reflects exasperation, contempt and tired resignation:
'You mistake me, my dear. I have a high respect for
your nerves. They are my old friends. I have heard you
mention them with consideration these twenty years at
least' (p. 6).

By contrast with Mr Bennet's terseness, Mr Collins is
incapable of employing one word if six will do. The
sense of his utterances is invariably self-regarding and
their construction is ponderous and in danger of losing
its way: 'If I,' said Mr Collins, 'were so fortunate as to
be able to sing, I should have great pleasure, I am sure,
in obliging the company with an air; for I consider
music as a very innocent diversion, and perfectly
compatible with the profession of a clergyman' (p. 85).

*Dialogue and
conversation*

Talk is central to Jane Austen's novels. It ranges from
passages of dialogue between intimates such as Jane and
Elizabeth to set piece conversations like those between
Elizabeth and Darcy at Netherfield. However, the novel
is not a play script because, in addition to their words,
we are presented with the characters' attitudes and
reactions.

Characters and caricatures

Jane Austen 'grades' her characters, as it were. Elizabeth is the most complex and we view her in close-up. Darcy is presented in rather less detail, whilst Jane and Bingley are even more straightforward. Much of the novel's interest and fun lies in the way these 'normal' characters come in contact with the caricatures (see Literary Terms), notably Mrs Bennet, Mr Collins and Lady Catherine.

Details

Pride and Prejudice is full of details that sum up a whole situation or character in a few words. Here are some examples:

- 'Mr Darcy said very little, and Mr Hurst nothing at all ... The latter was thinking only of his breakfast' (p. 30)
- 'Lady Lucas, who had been long yawning at the repetition of delights which she saw no likelihood of sharing, was left to the comforts of cold ham and chicken' (p. 84)
- 'In as short a time as Mr Collins long speeches would allow, everything was settled' (p. 102)
- 'Her home and her housekeeping, her parish and her poultry, and all their dependent concerns, had not yet lost their charms' (p. 178)

PART FOUR

STUDY SKILLS

HOW TO USE QUOTATIONS

One of the secrets of success in writing essays is the way you use quotations. There are five basic principles:
- Put inverted commas at the beginning and end of the quotation
- Write the quotation exactly as it appears in the original
- Do not use a quotation that repeats what you have just written
- Use the quotation so that it fits into your sentence
- Keep the quotation as short as possible

Quotations should be used to develop the line of thought in your essays.

Your comment should not duplicate what is in your quotation. For example:

Elizabeth thinks Jane is sweet, disinterested and angelic when she says 'Your sweetness and disinterestedness are really angelic'.

Far more effective is to write:

When Elizabeth tells Jane 'Your sweetness and disinterestedness are really angelic' she shows her concern that Jane is too good-natured and reticent.

However, the most sophisticated way of using the writer's words is to embed them into your sentence:

The 'wild giddiness' of Kitty and Lydia was just one example of the 'the folly and indecorum' of her family which made Elizabeth feel so ashamed.

When you use quotations in this way, you are demonstrating the ability to use text as evidence to support your ideas - not simply including words from the original to prove you have read it.

Everyone writes differently. Work through the suggestions given here and adapt the advice to suit your own style and interests. This will improve your essay-writing skills and allow your personal voice to emerge.

The following points indicate in ascending order the skills of essay writing:

- Picking out one or two facts about the story and adding the odd detail
- Writing about the text by retelling the story
- Retelling the story and adding a quotation here and there
- Organising an answer which explains what is happening in the text and giving quotations to support what you write

....

- Writing in such a way as to show that you have thought about the intentions of the writer of the text and that you understand the techniques used
- Writing at some length, giving your viewpoint on the text and commenting by picking out details to support your views
- Looking at the text as a work of art, demonstrating clear critical judgement and explaining to the reader of your essay how the enjoyment of the text is assisted by literary devices, linguistic effects and psychological insights; showing how the text relates to the time when it was written

The dotted line above represents the division between lower and higher level grades. Higher-level performance begins when you start to consider your response as a reader of the text. The highest level is reached when you offer an enthusiastic personal response and show how this piece of literature is a product of its time.

Coursework
essay

Set aside an hour or so at the start of your work to plan what you have to do.

- List all the points you feel are needed to cover the task. Collect page references of information and quotations that will support what you have to say. A helpful tool is the highlighter pen: this saves painstaking copying and enables you to target precisely what you want to use.
- Focus on what you consider to be the main points of the essay. Try to sum up your argument in a single sentence, which could be the closing sentence of your essay. Depending on the essay title, it could be a statement about a character: Although Charlotte's willingness to settle for the safety of 'a comfortable home' shocks Elizabeth, it was a wholly understandable decision for a twenty-seven-year-old woman with an uncertain future; an opinion about setting: The elegance of Pemberley's grounds reflects the good taste of its owner; or a judgement on a theme: In *Pride and Prejudice* Jane Austen demonstrates that happiness and harmony are achieved only if we are prepared to see ourselves, as well as others, with fresh eyes.
- Make a short essay plan. Use the first paragraph to introduce the argument you wish to make. In the following paragraphs develop this argument with details, examples and other possible points of view. Sum up your argument in the last paragraph. Check you have answered the question.
- Write the essay, remembering all the time the central point you are making.
- On completion, go back over what you have written to eliminate careless errors and improve expression. Read it aloud to yourself, or, if you are feeling more confident, to a relative or friend.

If you can, try to type your essay, using a word processor. This will allow you to correct and improve your writing without spoiling its appearance.

Examination essay

The essay written in an examination often carries more marks than the coursework essay even though it is written under considerable time pressure.

In the revision period build up notes on various aspects of the text you are using. Fortunately, in acquiring this set of York Notes on *Pride and Prejudice*, you have made a prudent beginning! York Notes are set out to give you vital information and help you to construct your personal overview of the text.

Make notes with appropriate quotations about the key issues of the set text. Go into the examination knowing your text and having a clear set of opinions about it.

In most English Literature examinations you can take in copies of your set books. This in an enormous advantage although it may lull you into a false sense of security. Beware! There is simply not enough time in an examination to read the book from scratch.

In the examination

- Read the question paper carefully and remind yourself what you have to do.
- Look at the questions on your set texts to select the one that most interests you and mentally work out the points you wish to stress.
- Remind yourself of the time available and how you are going to use it.
- Briefly map out a short plan in note form that will keep your writing on track and illustrate the key argument you want to make.
- Then set about writing it.
- When you have finished, check through to eliminate errors.

To summarise,
these are the
keys to success:

- Know the text
- Have a clear understanding of and opinions on the storyline, characters, setting, themes and writer's concerns
- Select the right material
- Plan and write a clear response, continually bearing the question in mind

SAMPLE ESSAY PLAN

A typical essay question on *Pride and Prejudice* is followed by a sample essay plan in note form. This does not present the only answer to the question, merely one answer. Do not be afraid to include your own ideas and leave out some of the ones in this sample! Remember that quotations are essential to prove and illustrate the points you make.

What part does Lady Catherine play in *Pride and Prejudice*?

Part 1
Introduction

Lady Catherine's role may be considered from three points of view:
- Her character and what it represents
- How she relates to other characters
- Her part in the development of the story

Part 2
Character

She represents undisguised pride at its most arrogant.

We initially learn of her from Mr Collins and she is first presented in the scenes at Rosings. Mr Collins's servility in itself suggests a woman who is excessively vain and self-important and this is confirmed in the way in which she soaks up compliments and dominates the conversation.

She has the inbred sense of superiority that is associated with her position in society. She is an old-world aristocrat who thinks she has the right to interfere in other people's lives such as those of her tenants and other local people and then later, Elizabeth's. This behaviour contrasts with Darcy's responsible sense of duty towards his tenants and employees.

Her vain pride is also reflected in her vulgarity and lack of taste, represented in the contrast between Pemberley with Rosings – her £800 fireplace is a sign of ostentatious wealth. Her professed love for music is a sham.

Her insolence towards Elizabeth shows lack of true breeding and shows her to be no more refined than Mrs Bennet at the other end of the social scale.

Part 3
Relationships

She brings out the best in Elizabeth first at Rosings and then later at Longbourn. Her arrogant pride which amounts to insolence contrasts with Elizabeth's integrity. We also see by *contrasting* the two characters that Elizabeth has superior intelligence and manners. At Rosings Darcy is embarrassed for Elizabeth by Lady Catherine's rudeness, just as Elizabeth had been embarrassed by her mother.

Part 4
Narrative role

She is the catalyst that finally brings Elizabeth and Darcy together, first by confronting Elizabeth then by reporting the interview to Darcy.

FURTHER QUESTIONS

Make a plan as shown above and attempt these questions.

1 What different aspects of marriage are presented in *Pride and Prejudice?*

2 Explain why Darcy's proposal is a turning point in the novel.

3 Why does her visit to Pemberley make such an impression on Elizabeth?

4 Give an account of Elizabeth's relationships with her family.

5 In what ways does Elizabeth show an independent mind?

6 What are Darcy's virtues?

7 How does Jane Austen show that Mrs Bennet is 'a woman of mean understanding, little information, and uncertain temper'?

8 What are Mr Bennet's strengths and weaknesses?

9 How does Jane Austen demonstrate that Mr Collins is 'a conceited, pompous, narrow-minded, silly man'?

10 In what ways is Wickham important to the plot and themes of *Pride and Prejudice*?

11 How do members of the Bennet family embarrass and shame Elizabeth?

12 How much sympathy can one have for Charlotte Lucas?

13 What does *Pride and Prejudice* tell us about life in early-nineteenth-century England?

14 The earliest form of the novel was called *First Impressions*. Do you think this would be a good title for the novel as we know it?

15 How are pride and prejudice related?

PART FIVE

CULTURAL CONNECTIONS

BROADER PERSPECTIVES

Like Mr Collins, Mr Elton in Emma *is another absurd clergyman, whilst his wife is as vulgar as Lady Catherine but more frighteningly real, and can be identified at any fashionable social gathering to this day!*

Jane Austen's output was quite small and once one is familiar with one novel, the others become wholly accessible. *Northanger Abbey* (Penguin Classics, 1996 – first published 1818) is an amusing reminder that the author had a tongue-in cheek attitude to the **romantic fiction** (see Literary Terms) on which her plots are based. It may be instructive to compare the lively Elizabeth with the rather more smug Emma in *Emma* (Penguin Classics, 1996 – first published 1816) or the more reflective Anne in *Persuasion* (Penguin Classics, 1996 – first published 1818).

It is instructive to compare Jane Austen's cool, witty presentation of romantic relationships with the more passionate visions of some of her contemporaries e.g. John Keats's poem, *The Eve of St Agnes* (1818) whose lovers, Madeline and Porhyro, are very different from Elizabeth and Darcy, or *Wuthering Heights* (Penguin Classics, 1995 – first published 1847) by another clergyman's daughter, Emily Brontë.

Jane Austen and her contemporaries established a tradition of conversational novels that is unbroken to this day in the works of Joanna Trollope, Mary Wesley, and especially Barbara Pym, who combines shrewd observation and gentle satire. One of her novels, *Some Tame Gazelle* (Jonathan Cape, 1950), even contains a proposal of marriage from another pompous and ridiculous clergyman.

Film and Television
There have been many adaptations of Jane Austen's novels.

The enormous popularity of the BBC version of *Pride and Prejudice* (1996) adapted by Andrew Davis and Emma Thompson's *Sense and Sensibility* (1996) is testimony to the enduring nature of the plots and they are useful at suggesting the sexual allure that lies below the surface poise and elegance.

anticlimax an often humorous effect created by the sudden descent from the important or high sounding to the trivial or banal. The effect is expressed in the phrase 'from the sublime to the ridiculous'

caricature [note the spelling] the presentation of character through the exaggeration of particular personality features, often used to ridicule failings such as vanity and pomposity

denouement the final unfolding of the plot enabling it to move towards its proper conclusion

irony (adj. ironic) basically saying one thing but meaning another, it can take many forms. An episode in the plot may be ironic because it has a significance not evident at the time or an expression may be ironic because it suggests other meanings than the literal sense

parody a conscious imitation of a style for comic effect

point of view a complex aspect of narrative that concerns whose thoughts or attitudes are being represented. They may be those of the character, the narrator, the author or the reader

Romantic(ism) a term relating to the artistic movement that began towards the end of the eighteenth century and stressed the importance of emotion and individual imagination

satire writing which exposes the follies of human behaviour by presenting it as absurd or ridiculous

romantic fiction (romance) a popular form of sentimental love story

wit a blend of humour, intelligence and verbal brilliance

TEST ANSWERS

TEST YOURSELF (Chapters 1–12)

A 1 Mr Bennet *(Chapter 1)*
2 Sir William Lucas *(Chapter 5)*
3 Mary Bennet *(Chapter 6)*
4 Charlotte Lucas *(Chapter 5)*
5 Charles Bingley *(Chapter 3)*

TEST YOURSELF (Chapters 13–23)

A 1 Elizabeth Bennet *(Chapter 16)*
2 Mrs Bennet *(Chapter 18)*
3 Mr Collins *(Chapter 18)*
4 Mr Collins *(Chapter 13)*
5 Miss de Bourgh *(Chapter 14)*
6 George Wickham *(Chapter 15)*

TEST YOURSELF (Chapters 24–38)

A 1 Jane *(Chapter 24)*
2 Mr Gardiner *(Chapter 25)*
3 Miss de Bourgh *(Chapter 28)*
4 Darcy *(Chapter 31)*

5 Darcy and Jane *(Chapter 33)*
6 Catherine (Kitty) and Lydia *(Chapter 37)*

TEST YOURSELF (Chapters 39–50)

A 1 Darcy's housekeeper (Mrs Reynolds) of Wickham *(Chapter 43)*
2 Caroline Bingley of Elizabeth *(Chapter 45)*
3 Jane of her father *(Chapter 47)*

TEST YOURSELF (Chapters 51–61)

A 1 Lydia to Jane *(Chapter 51)*
2 Elizabeth to Lydia *(Chapter 51)*
3 Elizabeth to Jane *(Chapter 54)*
4 Lady Catherine de Bourgh *(Chapter 56)*
5 Mr Bennet *(Chapter 57)*
6 Darcy *(Chapter 58)*